THE DEATH LIST

JACK CROSS SI6
BOOK 1

JACK DILLON

ROUGH
EDGES
PRESS

The Death List
Paperback Edition
Copyright © 2023 (As Revised) Jack Dillon

Rough Edges Press
An Imprint of Wolfpack Publishing
9850 S. Maryland Parkway, Suite A-5 #323
Las Vegas, Nevada 89183

roughedgespress.com

Paperback ISBN 978-1-68549-277-9
eBook ISBN 978-1-68549-276-2

THE DEATH LIST

PROLOGUE

APRIL 27

"Target in sight," Jack Cross said into his throat mic as he peered into the scope of his L129A1 Sharpshooter sniper rifle.

He didn't need a spotter for this shot; he was only one hundred and fifty yards out and could quite easily make it from there.

"Okay, Jack, take it easy. This is too quiet for me." Mike Flynn replied through the receiver in Jack's ear. "There should be others around."

"I like quiet; I'll take quiet from time to time—"

Suddenly all hell broke loose.

Bullets peppered the rooftop where he was lying from somewhere beneath him, kicking up clouds of dust and shattered pumice.

"Keep your head down!" Mike shouted.

"That thought had occurred to me," Jack quipped as he hunkered down behind the lip of the roof.

Another continuous burst of automatic weapons' fire

raked the lip of the roof close to where Jack lay, he was pinned down.

"A little help here!" Jack growled through the comm.

"Working on it," Mike replied breathlessly, his voice sounding labored in Jack's ear.

Jack knew that Mike was several yards away from his position overlooking the street, and it would take him several minutes before he was in any position to help. He just had to wait and survive.

A spatter of gunfire from the street below announced Mike's presence. The gunfire that had raked the rooftop had stopped. Taking a deep breath to steady himself, Jack held his rifle up to his shoulder, ready to fire.

Staring down the scope, he saw three gunmen pinned down behind a row of cars across the street from his position. They were taking cover from gunfire coming from somewhere down the street; Mike had arrived.

Taking quick aim, he fired three rapid shots. Each 7.62mm round struck its intended target, and the head of each gunman snapped back in a splash of blood and gore.

Jack scanned the rest of the street, keeping an eye out for any other hostiles.

Where is everyone? he wondered.

The street was reminding him of some post-apocalyptic movie. All that was required was a mob

Mike's voice came through the comm, "Let's get out of here, Jack,"

Suddenly gunfire raked the street directly in front of where Mike was standing. Jack looked on as his friend instantly reacted by diving to the side to avoid getting hit.

Jack pivoted his rifle around to where the gunfire originated, firing a couple of rounds for good measure.

For a second, the firing ceased, giving Mike the opportunity to gather himself and sprint for cover.

An open-top jeep came careering around the corner, nearly ejecting passengers in the process. In the back stood a tall man in military fatigues behind a mounted 50cal machine gun.

Jack saw the man's shoulders shudder as he took aim and began firing the weapon, sending a hail of large-caliber bullets down the street at Mike.

The driver's head exploded as the 7.62mm shell from Jack's rifle found its target, splattering the passengers with blood and brains before his body slumped forward over the steering wheel, dead.

The jeep careened over out of control, crashing into the side of buildings in a spectacular burst of white-hot flames.

Jack sprinted back to the roof's fire escape; ignoring the rungs, he opted for the faster way down and grasped the sides of the ladder, sliding to the street where Mike was waiting at the rear of the building. Making sure the coast was clear, they ran to the spot where they had parked their ride.

They drove in silence, each lost in their own thoughts of what had gone wrong and what they would report to their boss.

It wasn't long before they reached the clearing where their chopper was stashed. This was supposed to have been a quick in-and-out op, but it had rapidly gone tits up. Several goons were dead, and their target had been a no-show.

As the chopper climbed into the air, Jack said, "This is it, Mike. I'm done."

"Not again, Jack. You say that after every op," Mike replied, looking out the window. He didn't even bother looking at his friend, he'd heard this too many times before to give it any notice.

"I mean it this time, if I don't quit, then Melissa and me are through. I can't keep putting her through this; her not knowing if I'll come back every time I leave home is killing her. This one was too close; things went wrong from the start and could've been a whole lot worse."

"But they weren't because we're damn good at what we do."

"You're missing the point here, where was the target? We were supposed to make the hit on Escobar, one of the largest drug lords in the business. According to intel from MI6, he should've been there. Our intel was wrong, and we were very nearly screwed because of it, and no one would've known until it was too late."

"I see your point, but we knew the risks when we signed on. It's part of the job, and in this job, shit invariably happens."

"Well, maybe I'm fed up of getting covered in it."

"If you quit, what will you do, buddy, eh? You're not the nine-to-five type, and you know it."

"I'm going to have to learn then. When we get back, I'm handing in my notice."

Jack knew his friend was looking at him and knew what he was thinking because he was thinking it too. His job wasn't the type you could just quit. He had to try though, his family deserved better.

He turned and looked out the window, trying to picture what the future had in store.

CHAPTER ONE

THREE MONTHS LATER

When Mike received the call from General Donald Bainbridge, his first thought was: *I wonder whom I'll have to kill?*

He had worked for the man long enough to know it was not wise to be tardy. Punctuality was one of the General's watchwords, and being a military man, he ran his unit the same.

The unit in question was a covert tactical intelligence group that went by the name of Special Intelligence Section Six, often abbreviated to just SI6.

SI6 was set up after the 9/11 and subsequent 7/7 attacks to combat terrorism against the sovereign realm of Great Britain, and was answerable only to the Prime Minister of the day. This meant it had no political ties or bias. What it did have was an executive order to handle matters with extreme prejudice.

Within a year of its inception, SI6 had reduced acts of terrorism by a third, proving its effectiveness as a deterrent, and in doing so, earning itself a frightening reputation for being ruthlessly efficient.

SI6 was the third option against terrorism when diplomacy and military action had failed or weren't viable courses of action. The 'Third Option' meant taking the fight directly to terrorists in a cold and covert manner, secretly. They had to operate this way; if any of the missions ever saw the light of day, the government sanctioning them would be reviled as much as the terrorists they were sent to combat.

Headquarters was situated in an abandoned underground tube station that snaked beneath the streets of London. Access to it was from several locations, but the one Flynn would use was in a multi-story car park with a secret level concealed beneath it.

Mike had been a top operative for a number of years with SI6. He and Jack Cross had been an extremely successful team. Jack had been recruited from the British Special Air Service, while Mike was from the United States Special Forces branch that everyone denied existed, Delta Force. Ever since Jack had resigned though —something Mike still found remarkable he was finding it difficult to adjust to going solo.

Dressed in a dark blue suit with a white shirt and red silk tie, he drove his Alfa Romeo 146 through the tangled streets from his apartment with practiced ease until he reached the car park. As he drove past the guard post, the sentry on duty activated the entrance for him, lifting the barrier and allowing him to drive down the ramp to the extra level reserved for operatives and personnel.

Within a few moments, he was walking through the corridor leading to his destination, having passed through several security stops on the way in. He opened the door to the outer office and was greeted by the General's personal assistant Jennifer Austin, one of the most memorable women he'd ever met.

She was sitting behind her desk; her blonde hair fell around her shoulders like a cascade of sunlight. As she looked up to see who had entered, her sparkling ice-blue eyes shone, and her smile lit up her entire face.

"Hi, Mike."

The high cheekbones, the full sensuous lips, and the curve of her chin were just as he remembered from the first time he saw her. Jennifer Austin was an intelligence officer seconded from MI6. She had started in the military police, where she stayed for two years, after which she opted for a position in intelligence. After completing a year in Intel, she was seconded to MI6 for a mission, which she completed admirably. MI6 kept her on until Bainbridge asked for her personally to be his personal aide six months later. Not knowing who or what he was, she declined the position—until he filled her in as to what her duties would be and what the purpose of SI6 was. Now his office could not run without her invaluable input.

At the age of twenty-eight, she had the face and figure of a runway model ten years her junior. Her long blonde hair, ice-blue eyes that hinted at mischievousness, and full sensuous lips, were people's first impressions. If they lingered long enough, her long, slim legs and trim waist, topped off by a firm, well-rounded bosom, were bound to keep their attention. Many times, she'd used her stunning looks to disarm someone, once they realized the truth that it all came with a fierce intelligence, it was usually too late.

"Hi, Jen, you look as lovely as ever," he said, returning her smile.

"The General's expecting you; you'd better go straight in, sounds important," she said.

"Isn't it always?" he joked.

"Get in there before he comes after you," she said in all seriousness.

Without another word, he entered the inner sanctum of the General's office. The room was large, decorated in lush autumnal colors. A large Adam fireplace well stocked with wood was to his left. To his right was a solitary large paned window with a bookcase neatly stocked with leather-bound volumes.

At the far end of the room sat General Donald Bainbridge behind an imposing mahogany desk. On the wall behind him was a painting, a landscape by Turner. His desk was orderly, just like he ran the unit, and Flynn doubted his life was ever anything but.

He looked up from the file he was working on, "Come in, Flynn, be with you in a moment."

Bainbridge was a large, barrel-chested man with a military bearing, stiff back, and broad shoulders. He had a strong jawline, straight nose, and eyes that gave evidence of his fierce intelligence. His salt and pepper hair was cut short, exactly as it had always been throughout his military career. The suit he wore was a grey pinstripe, hand-tailored to fit his large frame. Exercise had been a big part of his life; he was fitter than most men half his age. Even though he was in his late fifties, he appeared at least a decade younger.

Finally, he finished up what he had been working on and closed the file. Looking up, he sat back and said, "Right, down to business, sit down, Flynn."

Flynn sat his six-foot frame down in the chair opposite, an air of expectation warming through him. His slate grey eyes were intense with concentration as he waited for the briefing on a new mission. He crossed his legs, attempting to appear cool and calm, a front that perhaps only a handful of people could see through, one of whom was the General. He knew the General would know that he was chomping at the bit about going back to work.

"You've heard of Frank Grogan," it was a statement rather than a question, for Grogan was one of the top ten most wanted terrorists.

"Yes, sir, of course," Flynn replied, his voice deep and warm.

"Well, we've been handed an opportunity to nab him," Bainbridge said with a slight smile. He knew that would spark his operative's interest.

Flynn uncrossed his legs and sat forward. "Really," he said.

"Really, a young hacker named Johnny Goff approached Grogan and offered him a list of covert agents' names; Goff was actually working for MI6 at the time," Bainbridge explained.

"He offered him a NOC list, why?" asked Flynn.

"Apparently, the young chap was disgruntled at how he had been recruited. He was caught hacking into government files, and rather than send him down for a stretch, they recruited him. He wasn't happy with the pay and conditions, being under scrutiny twenty-four-seven. I mean, for God's sake, what did he expect? That they would forgive him for all his sins? Anyway, this was his idea of getting back at the establishment. He obviously never thought they'd catch him," Bainbridge said.

"If Grogan got his hands on that, he could sell it to anyone in the world, then everyone on that list would be in danger."

"We think he already has a buyer in place. Grogan is

not the kind of man to set this up on his own. We think he's working under orders."

"Let me guess, Goff set up the meet for tonight," Flynn groaned.

"Correct. Grogan had contacted him to ask when he'd have the NOC list. Rather than let this go, they thought it best to go along," Bainbridge agreed.

"It's a bit short notice, isn't it, sir? Where did this come from, Goff's handler?"

"Sort of, I had a call from the Deputy Director, Stuart Tyler, who was handling the case. I can imagine he's quite keen to get this sorted fast before it leaks that a hacker they had working for them was willing to sell a NOC list right from under their noses. Because Six isn't supposed to mount operations on mainland Britain, he didn't want this chance to slip away. It's been handed over to Special Branch, but he wanted us along to ensure Grogan didn't get away."

"Sounds almost plausible, sir," replied Flynn skeptically, his eyebrows furrowing in thought.

"Yes, it does," Bainbridge agreed in the same tone.

"Do you believe him?"

"Not in the slightest. Tyler's bound to be up to something, but I'm not going to lose the chance of nabbing Grogan, so I want you up there just in case."

"I understand. He won't get away this time, sir."

"So far, this is the closest we've come to getting anywhere near him in the last two decades. If his reputation is anything to go by, he'll be prepared for anything. You're to offer your services to the Branch boys already in place on arrival. Do what you can to ensure Grogan comes back alive. If that's not an option though, I can quite easily live with him being dead."

"Copy that, I'll do my best, sir."

"I'm sure you will. Miss Austin will give you the address of Goff's house, then go visit the Armourer, I believe he has your new weapon ready."

"Goff's house? They set the meet up at his home?" Flynn asked, his eyebrows arching in surprise.

"Apparently so. Tyler thought they'd go along with the young chap's original plan. Any deviations at this late date would raise suspicions in Grogan."

"Yes, sir."

"That's all. Good luck," Bainbridge said. He reached for another file, opened it, and began writing; the briefing clearly was at an end.

Flynn got to his feet and left the room.

Jennifer Austin was waiting for him with Johnny Goff's address the moment he left Bainbridge's office.

"Here's the address you need, Mike. You'd better be off, the Armourer is waiting for you," she said with some urgency.

"What's the rush?"

"Check the address; it must be at least a two-hour drive. You don't want the Branch boys taking you for one of the bad guys and shooting you on sight," she explained with a grin.

Flynn read the address and nodded in agreement.

"I'll see you when I get back. This shouldn't take too long," he said.

"Mike, be careful," she said with a worried expression.

He looked up from the address and gave her a smile of such charm that most women would have melted before it, but not Jennifer, she had seen it all before.

"I'll be okay, don't worry."

"Oh, don't think I'll be worried, I just don't want all the extra paperwork, that's all," she said coldly, but her eyes and smile said otherwise.

"Ah, my heart's just broken. I thought you had a soft spot for me."

"I do, it's a bog in Ireland! Now go on get out of here before the Armourer phones through to the General to see where you are."

Flynn laughed, then waved to her and left.

As he closed the door behind him, her expression altered, a fleeting look of intense concern crossed her beautiful face before she composed herself, put her worries away, and got on with her job.

———

The Armourer was, in fact, Major Arthur Bacon, a thirty-year veteran who had worked with the SAS in various capacities until Bainbridge seconded him to work with the agents to make sure their equipment and weapons were top-notch and would never let them down. He was close to retirement age, with most of his dark hair turned white. There was an aura of restless energy about him, his wiry five-foot-ten frame always on the move. He had a broken nose from his days in the Army boxing team, but that was the only visible scar. A master of weaponry, he was ideal for his duties.

The basement was where he was stationed. There were firing ranges where personnel could practice with and get used to different firearms, and where the Major could conduct tests upon the weapons before issuing them to the agents.

Flynn took the elevator down to the basement, as the doors opened, he was greeted by the sight of Major Bacon obviously waiting for him.

"What kept you, Flynn? I was told you'd be here a

while ago. I thought this was an urgent case," he said sarcastically.

"I got here as soon as I could, Major, sir," Flynn replied, standing to attention.

"Cut the sarcasm, Flynn." He chastised before turning towards the interior of his base of operations. "Down to business. Here's your new weapon." The Major handed over the Beretta Cougar 8000 to Flynn, who hefted it in his right hand, feeling the balance.

Looking at the pistol, he nodded his head in satisfaction, smiling.

"Nice one, Major. I've never tried this model before," he said as he picked up a magazine and inserted it into the butt, ramming it into place with the palm of his hand. Pulling back on the slide, he injected a round into the chamber, ready for firing, before asking, "May I?"

"Feel free," Bacon replied, picking up a set of hearing protectors and passing them to Flynn. As Flynn took them, Bacon placed another set around his own ears and followed Flynn over to one of the firing ranges.

In the proper firing stance, Flynn fired his weapon rapidly three times at the man-shaped target down the range. Taking aim again, he fired two more shots and then put down the weapon.

Major Bacon operated the winch bringing the target up the range so they could view his efforts.

As the target grew nearer, they could see that the first salvo of three shots was tightly grouped in the circle of the heart. The second salvo of two shots had been a double tap to the center of the forehead, dead center above the eyes.

"I think it'll be fine," Flynn said with a deadpan expression.

"Remarkable," muttered Bacon, who always marveled

at the casual ease with which Flynn operated his weapon with such deadly accuracy. He had heard tales of Flynn's dead-eye accuracy under fire from other agents, although he'd never seen it personally. Usually, when an agent is in a life-or-death situation, the accuracy deteriorates somewhat. There are some who perform well under conditions of extreme stress, and a rare few who perform better under those conditions, Flynn was one of those rare few. He was ice cool under pressure, so much so that those who had witnessed him in action wondered if ice water ran through his veins rather than blood.

"If that's all, Major, then I'll be off, sir," Flynn said, retrieving his weapon from the bench as Bacon scrutinized the target once more.

"No, that's all, Flynn, dismissed," he replied to the retreating form already heading for the elevator.

CHAPTER TWO

Flynn drove his Alfa 146 from the car park and out into the city traffic.

The address he'd been given was the Glades, Nr. Buxton. It was a detached converted farmhouse that was set back from the road.

Slowing down, he pulled into the curb behind the Transit and parked up. He switched off the engine and got out of the car.

The moment his car door closed, someone got out of the Transit van and began walking toward him.

"Hold it right there," the man said in a commanding voice. He was tall, at least as tall as Flynn, and lean. Dressed in a polo shirt, jeans, and trainers, with a leather bomber jacket on top, he looked nothing like a Special Branch officer, but Flynn was pleased to notice they had come prepared for trouble.

"Who're you, and what's your business here, sir?" the man demanded.

Flynn held his hands away from his body to clearly show he was holding nothing.

"I've been sent to help you with Grogan," he said.

The Special Branch officer reached for his pistol, a Browning hi-power nine millimeter automatic, and snapped into the marksman's stance aiming directly at Flynn's face.

"Right, freeze," he ordered. "How do you know of Grogan?" he added warily, casting glances into Flynn's car to see if there was anyone else concealed inside. He looked around him also to see if the man before him was a decoy.

"I work for the same people you do. I've been ordered to render any assistance I can," Flynn replied calmly. "Have you a cell phone with you?" he asked.

"Why?" the Special Branch officer asked, puzzled.

"I have a number you can call for all the verification you require," Flynn replied without a trace of concern.

"Why would the Ministry send anyone here, this is a Branch matter now?" argued the officer.

"Make the call," Flynn urged with a trace of steel in his voice.

"I rather think you're a decoy sent to distract us from our objective. Move towards the van," ordered the officer.

"You're making a mistake," Flynn said.

"Move it, now," the officer clipped through clenched teeth.

Flynn moved forward, and as he got closer, he grabbed the officer's wrist holding the Browning, fluidly twisting it in a painful grasp until he released his grip on it. In less than a second, Flynn had the pistol aimed at its owner.

"Now, shall we make that call before someone gets hurt?" Flynn asked.

———

Overlooking the farmhouse at the rear, Frank Grogan watched through his night vision binoculars. Everything around the house was illuminated as if it was daytime but tinted green.

He had arrived earlier that day, driving past the house and the ford Transit, which was already on station, parked outside the safe house. Driving past at a steady pace, he had noticed two men in the front cabin and another walking down the path towards the rear of the house.

This smacked of an official babysitting op, but why would Goff have minders? He wondered. He could only think of one reason, the little bastard had sold him down the river.

Not to worry, he would take care of them and then take care of Goff. Once he had what he wanted from him, he'd make the little gobshite wish he'd never seen him.

Taking out his mobile phone, he called a number.

"Okay, Niall, it looks like I've been set up," he said.

"What're you gonna do then, Frank?" replied his friend.

"The sensible thing would be to walk away, but when have you ever known me to do the sensible thing?" Frank chuckled. He was enjoying this. Back when he was running the streets of his native Belfast, he made his name running rings around the Garda. He would make hits right under their noses. This would be no different. Just like old times.

———

Mike transferred a number from his phone to the Special Branch officer's phone.

"That number will give you the answers you're looking for," Mike told him.

The officer, still quite shaken by the speed he'd been disarmed, looked at his phone and the number on the screen.

"Okay," he said and dialed the number.

"Yes?" enquired a voice impatiently.

"Who is this?" the officer asked haltingly.

"General Bainbridge. Who the hell are you, sir, and how did you get this number?" Bainbridge snapped back.

"Inspector Hewitt of the Special Branch, sir."

"Special branch 'eh, I see. Is there someone there with you, six feet or so, slate grey eyes, dark hair, charming smile? He's probably holding your own gun on you as we speak."

"I can't testify to the smile, sir, but the rest is true."

"Yes, the insufferable chap works for me here at the MOD. You may have heard of us, SI6? We've been asked to liaise with you by Stuart Tyler, Deputy Director of MI6, just to help out."

"SI6, yes, sir, I've heard of you, but I thought you boys were a myth," Hewitt said with a raised eyebrow.

"I can assure you, Inspector, we are real, as is the job we do," Bainbridge said proudly.

"I see, sir," Hewitt replied and swallowed hard. He realized two things, and neither of them pleasant: the man in front of him was authentic, and this job was going to be much harder than they had been told.

"Good night, Inspector. Oh, and tell him to give you back your gun," Bainbridge said before hanging up his phone.

Hewitt looked at Mike as he put away his phone. "He says you're to give me my gun back."

Mike smiled and returned the Browning to him butt first.

"Right, what have we got here so far?" he asked.

CHAPTER THREE

Frank made his way down from his position on the top of the small rise behind Goff's house.

He'd already scouted out the location earlier when he'd had Niall Quinn, his best friend and right-hand man, drop him off in the layby past the farmhouse.

There was a tall fence that ran around the rear of the property, he climbed that with ease. Once he was in the garden, he could see quite clearly the French doors that led from the patio at the back of the house and into the kitchen beyond.

There were no security measures to speak of. Out here in the rural areas, crime was not the problem as it was in the towns and cities. People here still went to bed at night and left their doors unlocked.

This attitude suited Frank down to the ground as he had the French doors open in a flash.

Closing the door silently behind him, he reached into the waistband of his jeans at the small of his back for his Walther PPK with the Carswell silencer attached. He jacked the slide to inject a round into the breach and held it out in front of him.

Listening for any signs that he'd been made before he slowly began to make his way into the modern kitchen.

It was a tidy, well-thought-out room with cupboards to the side and above the work area, which included the cooker. On the opposite side was the sink next to the washer, dryer, and dishwasher. Beyond this was a dining room which led through an archway into the lounge.

A burly man dressed in a tee shirt and jeans appeared in the archway. Frank recognized him instantly as a minder.

The man's eyes went wide in surprise as he spotted the intruder. Reflexively he reached for a gun at his hip but was dead before he could clear his holster. The two bullets from Frank's gun hit him center mass in a mist of blood, sending him flying back against the wall. The shots the Walther emitted made no more noise than a slight coughing sound. The body hitting the wall before collapsing to the floor was far louder.

"What is it?" a voice shouted from inside the lounge.

Frank saw the young hacker come through from the lounge to investigate. He saw the fear in his eyes and the color drain from his already pale face at the sight of the man standing in his kitchen brandishing a pistol.

"Holy shit!" Goff exclaimed as he ran for the door that led upstairs.

Frank fired after him, the two bullets striking the door as Goff flung it wide in his haste to get away.

"Holy shit!" Goff exclaimed once more as he ran headlong up the stairs, heading for a room he hoped would offer him sanctuary until help arrived.

———

Flynn was out of the van and sprinting for the house the moment he heard Goff shout.

He snatched his Beretta from the soft leather holster beneath his left armpit and jacked the slide as he ran.

He was good to go.

The second he stepped foot in the kitchen, his fears that Grogan had been there were affirmed. The tell-tale trace of cordite in the air told him shots had been fired. The blood and the dead guard came as no surprise.

The thud of steps pounding upstairs drew his attention, and he realized that was where Goff had fled. He knew Grogan wouldn't be far behind, which meant Mike was rapidly running out of time.

Moving as fast as he could, he ran for the landing door.

————

Goff was screaming for help as he slammed the bedroom door behind him, struggling to lock it as fast as he could before jumping and sliding across the king-sized bed to unlatch the windows. Opening the windows wide, he shouted to the Branch minders that he was there.

He had never been so terrified in his entire life. Not even when he was arrested for hacking into government databases and was threatened with jail. Somehow he knew that they would've offered him some sort of deal, and there was never any real threat of him doing time, but this...this was real...he was in danger of being killed here.

He heard Grogan reach the locked door and throw himself against it.

It held, thankfully.

He knew it wouldn't stop that lunatic for long though.

He flinched as he heard the sound of three bullets striking the door around the lock.

Grogan kicked the damaged lock, and with a loud 'crash,' the door was flung open.

Goff saw Grogan standing in the doorway, and it was like looking at the Devil himself. He was average height and build, no taller than five feet eleven, and dressed in blue jeans and a black leather bomber jacket. His black hair was unkempt and grew down to his eyes and almost over his ears. It looked like it hadn't been washed in several days. He had a grin on his chiseled features that said he'd won, but no mirth showed in his dark eyes, which were so deep it was like looking into the pits of hell itself.

"Knock knock," he heard him say before adding, "Mind if I come in?I It's time to die."

———

Mike was halfway up the stairs when he heard the door give way.

Hang on, he prayed silently, *just a little longer.*

CHAPTER FOUR

"Get away from me, you bastard," Goff screamed in terror as Grogan stepped inside the room and raised his gun to fire.

"This is the price you pay for trying to stitch me up," Frank said coldly.

He aimed his Walther at Goff's head and pulled the trigger. Nothing happened. The slide had locked open, it was empty. In all the excitement, he had emptied his clip.

The look on his face was one of total shock. How had he not kept track of how many shots he'd fired?

Goff nearly pissed his pants out of terror and relief, then another voice joined the room.

"Freeze, Grogan!" the stranger's steely voice ordered.

———

Mike noted the pistol in Grogan's hand and knew it was empty.

He had the drop on him, but that wouldn't stop him

from doing something stupid like trying to fight his way out of this.

The young hacker was crouched into a ball behind the bed on the far side of the bedroom, cowering away from the terrorist.

Distracted for a second, Mike missed Grogan turning to throw his pistol at him.

He just had time to duck before it flew past his head, and Grogan made a dash for the open window.

By the time he had his Beretta back up to fire, Grogan was through the window.

Mike catapulted himself onto, then over, the bed to stand next to the window where Goff cowered.

"Stay there," he yelled as he vaulted through the window and onto the low roof of the kitchen. He spotted Grogan as he landed in a crouch on the back garden lawn. Taking advantage of the situation, Mike dove full length at the man tackling him in a bone-jarring collision, which sent both men tumbling to the ground.

As the momentum of their tandem roll slowed, Grogan seized the opportunity to press his advantage. Straddling Mike, he delivered a sharp punch to his stomach, then rose to run.

Staying calm as his lungs burned, Mike reached for the fleeing man, barely grasping him by the ankle, tripping him up and sending him crashing to the ground again.

"You don't get away that easily," Mike grunted. Righting himself, he got to his feet and noticed his Beretta lying on the ground just out of his reach. Grogan saw it as well as he staggered to his feet. If he wanted to get the gun before Mike, he would have to go through him first.

Grogan growled, "You've got spirit, I'll give you that,

but it's not enough to see you through this boyo."

Mike waited for the opportunity to take this man down, blocking the few jabs Grogan threw as he waited for him to make his move.

His opportunity finally came. Mike was ready for the low kick to the shins, easily blocking the blow with his foot. As the block connected, throwing Grogan off balance, he delivered a vicious right cross that sent Grogan staggering, followed by a square shot straight to the jaw that knocked him flat on his back.

"You were saying?" Mike said, standing over him.

As Mike stepped back, Grogan jumped up, intending to rush him. Reflexively Mike struck out with a side kick that slammed into his attacker, forcing the air from his chest with a 'whoosh!' stopping him dead in his tracks as he bent over, gasping for air. In one final strike, Mike stepped forward, bringing his right knee up into Grogan's face with a 'crunch', the force of the blow once more sending the man sprawling.

Mike calmly walked over to retrieve his Beretta, then returned to stand over Grogan as he attempted to get to his feet.

"I wouldn't if I were you, Frank. I've been ordered to bring you in, it didn't state you had to be breathing," Mike said coldly as he aimed his gun at the still struggling Grogan's head.

Grogan looked up at him, his eyes streaming, then spat a gob of blood and broken teeth on the ground as Mike allowed him to slowly get up.

A few moments later, Mike was dragging Grogan towards the path when he noticed Inspector Hewitt and another Special Branch officer approaching with incredulous expressions on their faces.

"You got him!" Hewitt exclaimed as if he hadn't

thought it possible.

"Yeah, now he's all yours, Inspector," Mike replied.

———

The two men Niall Quinn had brought with him were seated in a blue Mondeo at the front of the pub down the road from the house.

They had waited and watched the proceedings. Vickers, the driver, was a career criminal from Belfast as was his passenger, Lee Shaw.

Niall called Vickers on his mobile, putting it on speaker so they could both listen.

"Something's wrong. Go check it out but be careful," Niall said.

As they pulled off from the car park, Shaw pulled out a Browning 9mm and pulled back on the slide.

"Drive slowly up to the van, let's see what's going on," he said.

Vickers said nothing, just kept his dark eyes on the Transit as he drove forward slowly.

As they neared the van, Shaw spotted Grogan being shepherded down the path. He wound his window down, held his Browning through it, and shouted, "Frank!"

———

Mike and the others looked in the direction the shout came from just as a gunshot rang out and the lead man was sent sprawling as the round hit him.

Chaos ensued. Grogan shoved himself away from Hewitt as another shot rang out, sending Hewitt spinning as the bullet hit him high on his chest.

There was nothing Mike could do but watch and

wait. He was stuck behind the two Special Branch offi-cers—one dead and Hewitt wounded—as Grogan was off and running towards the car at the roadside.

Here was the backup for Grogan Mike had mentioned earlier to Hewitt.

The remaining Branch officers were trapped inside the van, unable to come to their aid.

Mike pushed past the two men and ran down the path after Grogan. He was directly behind the fleeing terrorist, so he knew those in the car couldn't get a clear shot at him just yet. That would change the moment Grogan reached them though.

Mike was prepared for the moment Grogan dove through the open window of the rear passenger door. The second Grogan leaped, he fired two shots straight at the man aiming the Browning at him from the front passenger seat, long before the man had a clear shot at him and a chance to pull the trigger. Both bullets struck their target with precision splattering the driver with brains and blood as the side of the man's head exploded from the dual impacts.

He heard Grogan scream, "Get us the fuck out of here!" as the driver slammed his foot down on the accelerator.

As the car fish-tailed, gaining speed, Mike knew he had seconds left before he lost them. With a Herculean effort, he increased his pace and flung himself at the fleeing vehicle. He landed, barely able to grab hold of the roof. Frantically, he pulled his right leg up on the rear of the vehicle, gaining better purchase.

Inside the vehicle, Mike heard the driver shout, "Who the fuck is this guy?"

Grogan angrily spat, "Just lose this prick." From the sound of it, Grogan was still lying across the back seats.

Knowing he had to incapacitate the driver, Mike shuffled himself into a better position where he could fire a salvo of five shots through the roof into the driver's side. He heard a cry of pain and knew he had hit pay dirt.

The sound of the shots startled Grogan, but it was Vickers who jumped when bullets met flesh in his shoulder and thigh until the last slug dug deep into his brain and he slumped hard against the steering wheel—his dead weight causing his foot to press hard against the accelerator.

———

Grogan was a dead man if he didn't regain control of the car, there was a bend coming, he just had to maneuver around it somehow. If he could, he just might get out of this alive. Quinn wasn't far away, he knew he was waiting; he just had to get there in one piece.

Reaching over the seat in front of him, he struggled to pull Vickers' dead body off the wheel so he could grab it one-handedly while the other steadied the body.

When they hit the bend, the back end of the car skidded, fish-tailing dangerously as Grogan wrestled with the steering wheel to regain control.

———

Mike held on for dear life as the car bucked and jerked under him as they skidded dangerously around the bend. He had to give Grogan credit, the man may be an ass, but he could drive.

Without warning, the car hit a bump, bounced, lost traction, and crashed through a fence—plummeting down a steep gradient to the valley below.

As the car picked up speed, Mike shoved himself away from the careering vehicle into the air and then landed hard as his momentum continued his descent, rolling uncontrollably until finally, he managed to slow then stop.

When the car bounced and headed for the fence, Grogan was tossed around in the back like a rag doll. He knew he had to escape, or his fate was sealed inside this car.

Lashing out, he kicked the door repeatedly until finally, with one last kick, it flew open.

"Oh Frank, this is gonna hurt," he mumbled as he prepared to jump, reminding himself, "Just go limp, just go limp." He flung himself from the careering vehicle, barely clearing it as it continued its headlong plunge toward the valley below.

Mike made his way down the slope as he watched Grogan fight his way free from the speeding car.

He walked down the slope and noticed Grogan as he watched the car slow to the bottom and gently come to a stop.

"Well, that was a bit of a let-down," Mike said softly. Grogan turned at the sound and was met full in the face by a straight right that put him on his back, again.

Grogan looked up at him, spat blood, and snarled, "Why don't you just fuck off and die?"

"Not today, Frank," Mike said as he aimed his Beretta at Grogan's face.

"And certainly not before you," he added with a straight face.

"You got him!" Hewitt's voice reached him as he approached down the bank.

Keeping his attention on Grogan, he became aware of Hewitt and another Special Branch officer as they came to stand next to him.

"He's all yours, and I think this time there'll be no interference," Mike said as the other officer snapped handcuffs on Grogan and roughly hauled him to his feet.

"You look terrible," he said, observing Hewitt's hand on the wound near his shoulder. The Inspector's fingers were slick with his own blood, and tell-tale evidence of pain was etched across his face.

"I've had better days," Hewitt replied through gritted teeth.

"Get that seen to before you head back. You need to take Goff with you as well; he'll need to face charges of treason. Will you be able to manage?"

"You've done enough, we can handle the rest from here, thanks," Hewitt replied painfully.

———

Niall Quinn had witnessed the entire scene.

What the fuck went wrong? He wondered as he continued to watch.

He fought an urge to attack and free Frank, but he contented himself with doing nothing but watch.

Live to fight another day, he reminded himself as he started up his car.

As he headed off towards the small market town of Buxton, he said, "Don't worry Frank my boyo, they won't keep you for long, that I promise."

CHAPTER FIVE

During the long drive back to London, Mike went over the days' events in his mind. Certain Hewitt would cope with the men he had guarding Grogan and Goff, he pulled out his mobile and voice dialled the office. Jen answered on the second ring.

"Inform the General that the mission was a success. Grogan is in custody and on his way back to London along with Goff," he said.

"Well done, Mike. I'll let the Old Man know he'll have your full report tomorrow," she replied.

"Thanks, I'll see you later," he said, ending the call.

Thinking twice before putting his phone away, he once again pressed the call button, instructing the phone to 'call Jack'. When a familiar voice answered, he said, "Hi, Jack, how's things?"

"Mike, hi mate, we're doing good, thanks. What've you been up to, getting into more trouble, I presume?" Jack Cross replied half-jokingly.

"Sort of, you know how work is. I just thought I'd call

to see how you and the family are and to see if we're still on for our regular boy's night?"

"We're fine, Mike. I've already told you that, and yes, if you're free, then our night is still on. Are you okay? What's wrong, you rarely call just for a chat?" Jack asked.

"Do you regret it, buddy, any of it? I know why you left, I get that, but what we did, what I still do, do you regret any of it? Do you think we did any good?" Mike asked, the words tumbling out before he had even thought about it.

"You're returning from an op, aren't you? And it was probably a bad one. Listen, you know we can't talk about this on an open line, but I'll say this, we did good. I know it's hard to see that sometimes, but I know we did good."

"You're right, it's sometimes just so damn hard to see that, you know?"

"I do, and I have to think that, Mike, because the alternative is unthinkable. What you have to decide now is, do you want to continue or leave like I did? If you want to leave, then leave, but if you decide to stay, do it for the right reasons. I've seen too many people stay in a job because they have nothing else and they burn out, I'd hate to see you end up like that," Jack told him. There was a pause, then Jack continued, "You're driving, I can tell. Just get back to base safely and I'll see you later in the week. We can talk then, okay?"

"Thanks, buddy. I knew I could rely on you."

———

In his office, Bainbridge had been waiting for the call as he worked through some files on his computer.

Jen gave him the run down as he listened intently. "Good work on Flynn's part. I look forward to reading his report. I'd better inform Tyler of the results, he'll want to keep Goff someplace safe until the trial. Grogan has a network of allies who'll be gunning for Goff."

"Right away, sir," Jen replied. Seconds later, her voice came through the intercom, informing him, "Stuart Tyler for you, sir," before transferring the call through to his extension.

"Good evening, Stuart. I trust I find you well," Bainbridge said.

"Very, thank you. Can this wait until morning? I was just about to leave for dinner." Tyler replied, clearly not wanting to talk.

"Sorry to hold you up, but you should know that Frank Grogan is in the custody of your Special Branch detail. It seems it was a wise move on your part to ask my unit for assistance, as my man's intervention was crucial. You should probably make arrangements concerning Goff and Grogan as soon as possible though," Bainbridge continued, not in the least concerned that he was ruining Tyler's plans for the evening.

"I'll get right on that, Donald, and thank you for being discrete in this matter. Six could have incurred irreparable damage if Goff's plans had been leaked. I owe you lunch at the very least, your choice. You just mention the place and the time, and I'll sort everything out," Tyler said, the impatience having left his voice.

"I'll keep you to that, Stuart," Bainbridge said, hanging up the phone.

He sat back and looked at the clock on his computer. A smile softened his normally stern features as he closed his computer down.

"Dinner sounds like an excellent idea," he said.

———

Niall Quinn was driving with the flow of the traffic when his mobile rang, scaring the shit out of him.

"Holy Mother of God, Niall, my boy, get a fucking grip," he exclaimed as he tried to compose himself.

Placing his Bluetooth headset on his ear and activating it, he said, "Who's this?"

The electronically altered voice on the other end replied, "If you want to help your friend, then listen carefully."

Warily Niall said, "Go on, I'm listening."

"Goff will be moved to a safe house while they wait for the trial. Everything hinges on that young man's testimony."

"How does that help me?"

"I'll give you the location of that safe house, the rest is up to you."

"And how do I know you're not working with Goff? He set us up; they were waiting for us when we got there. How do I know you're not trying to set me up the same way?"

"You don't. Do you want to take the chance and free your friend, or are you going to be a chicken shit coward who sits on his hands while your friend goes away for a very long time?"

Niall didn't have a choice. If the roles were reversed, Frank wouldn't hesitate, so he couldn't sit back and do nothing. He had to at least try.

"Okay, I see your point. Go ahead."

CHAPTER SIX

Mike returned to his office, tired from his earlier exertions.

He decided to fill out his report now, while it was still fresh in his mind. At least that way, he would get a decent night's sleep.

It was after midnight by the time he'd finished it and emailed it to the General's secure mailbox. His stomach growled loudly, reminding him he hadn't eaten since that morning. "I'd better do something about that," he mumbled to himself as he rose.

As he closed his door to the office, he heard a familiar deep, resonant voice behind him.

"Back so soon? Everything went well, I presume."

Mike turned to see the Chief of Staff, Colonel Anthony Armstrong, standing by the door to his own office. The Colonel was tall and lean, with short dark hair and deep brown eyes, which held a warmth that belied the cold, hard, ruthless quality he held in check. He had been the General's right-hand man for many years and a close family friend who had helped during the most traumatic time of his life.

The General, his wife, and their daughter had been targeted by a terrorist group one night when they went for dinner. Had it not been for the timely intervention of Armstrong's arrival, every single one of them would have died. As it was, the General's wife and daughter had been gunned down outside the restaurant they were visiting. The General, although badly wounded himself, managed to take out two of the four assailants, and Armstrong got the last just as he was about to shoot the General in the back of his head.

Shortly after that, Bainbridge had taken command of SI6 and had insisted Tony come with him as his Chief of Staff.

Armstrong was an amiable and approachable man, very easy to talk to.

"Oh, hi, Tony. I thought I was the only one here," Mike said with a tired smile.

"I was just finishing some reports. I didn't fancy coming in tomorrow. God, you look like shit, man. You look like you could do with a drink," Tony said with concern etching his brow.

"I'm starving. I can't remember when I last had a bite to eat."

"Come on, dinner's on me. You can tell me all about your trip, where was it? The back of beyond?"

"The Staffordshire moorlands, Tony. You do realize there's more of this country once you get past Watford?" joked Mike.

"I doubt it very much, but that's for another debate. Let's get some decent grub and a few drinks inside of you," Tony said with a broad smile.

CHAPTER SEVEN

Quinn returned to the tiny hotel he shared with Frank.

It was a fleabag really, frequented by whores and drug dealers, but it served their purpose—no one would look for them there.

He was in possession of the address where Goff was being held, a gift from their new unknown benefactor. He was troubled by this information—why should he trust this man, or the information he provided?

He truly only trusted one man, and he was now incarcerated. There were too many new faces around now, and he didn't trust any of them, so whatever he planned to do with this new information, he was certain he would have to do it alone.

Should he even do anything with this information? Maybe he should just sit back and stay safe?

What would Frank do?

That was a simple, he would act, and to hell with the consequences. It wasn't that he was rash, just the opposite. No one who acted rashly in this business ever lasted very long. No, he wouldn't be rash, but Frank did value friendship and loyalty. Above all, he valued his friendship and loyalty. Had the roles been reversed, there was no question in his mind Frank would act, so he would do the same.

He would have to do this alone though. Seeing as how he couldn't trust any of the others and it was too late to recruit anyone else now, this would have to be a solo mission.

With a clear direction set in his mind, he undressed and climbed into bed. Closing his eyes, he cleared his mind, within seconds, he was fast asleep.

———

"Good work Mike," Tony said once the waiter had cleared their plates away.

"Just doin' my job. Let's hope they can keep him locked up for good this time," Mike replied wearily. He put a hand over his mouth, stifling a yawn.

"Have faith, Mike, have faith. Now tell me, when was the last time you had any leave?" Tony queried, noticing the dark rings around his friend's eyes.

"A month or two, why?" he lied.

"Let's try over nine months, shall we? You haven't been on leave since Jack was with us," Tony corrected.

"You know how the Old Man likes to keep us busy," Mike replied flippantly.

"There's busy, and there's burnt out. I don't want you in the latter category. Therefore, I'm ordering you to take two weeks paid holiday, or as you Yanks call it, a vacation. As of now, you're on holiday. I've booked you on a flight to Iraklion airport, it leaves at seven-thirty tomorrow morning; sorry, this morning," Tony said with a glance at his Tag Heuer wristwatch. "Ever been to Crete before, Mike?"

"No, but it seems I'm about to," Mike replied with an arched eyebrow.

"You'll stay with a friend of mine, he'll look after you. Get some rest, Mike, you've earned it," Tony said.

Mike looked at his friend, the Colonel, and realized just how bone tired he was. Tony was right. He was in serious danger of burning out. He had missed vital things during this last mission, things that could have cost lives. One Special Branch officer was dead, another wounded. If he'd been at the top of his game, none of that would've happened.

Tony was right. He would take the time off. He'd been working non-stop for nearly a year. Two weeks of lounging by the pool, soaking up some sun suddenly seemed like an excellent idea.

With a smile, he said, "Seeing as how you put it like that, sir, how can I refuse?"

"You'll have the time of your life, Mike. Crete's a wonderful place; the people are friendly, and the food is wonderful. The rest will do you a world of good."

"What about Grogan?" Mike asked.

"We've done our bit; it's over to the Crown Prosecution Service now to make a case against him. I'm sure, considering the circumstances, this will be given priority status and rushed through the courts. With a bit of luck, it'll be all over by the time you return."

"You're right, and I'm sure they'll want to keep Goff's involvement under wraps too, but that's no longer my problem."

"Okay then, off you go. Go get packed and get yourself to the airport, you can grab a few hours kip on the plane. Next time I see you, I want to see you fully rested with a healthy tan," Tony said with a smile as he waved him off.

Mike pushed himself wearily to his feet. "Thanks again for the meal, Tony, and for the leave. I'll see you in two weeks," he said, then headed for the door.

CHAPTER EIGHT

"Are you sure I'll be safe here?" Goff asked, still shaken from his ordeal the night before.

He had been stuck in a holding cell overnight like a common criminal. *Outrageous,* he thought. He had done nothing really wrong apart from that little thing with Grogan and the NOC list, but they forced him into doing it. If they hadn't forced him into working for them, then none of this would've happened. So in actual fact, all of this was their fault. He was a free spirit, an anarchist fighting against government oppression. *I mean, let's face it, forcing someone like that into working for the very government he was against, what did they think would happen?*

"That's why it's called a safe house," replied Officer James Walker sarcastically, rolling his eyes in exasperation at his partner, Philip Trent.

Goff had been picked up by them early this morning at the police station, they'd been tasked with keeping him safe for the duration.

He'd been with them for less than an hour, and already they knew this was going to be a long day.

"It's just an ordinary house though," Goff whined from the back seat of the car.

"It has a state-of-the-art security suite, surveillance cameras that give a three-sixty degree view around the property, the doors are all reinforced, and the alarm system has motion sensors. It is also wired directly to HQ so that should anything happen, backup will get here within eight minutes," replied Walker.

Trent added, "So you see, there's nothing to worry about. You're in good hands, now c'mon, let's get inside."

"We'll go on in, you park the car around back," Walker told his partner.

Goff gingerly followed closely behind officer Walker as they entered the house, clearly still not convinced.

———

Mike was seated comfortably in first class, relaxing with a nicely aged Glenlivet single malt scotch as his flight left British airspace. The last nine months or so had been hard work, harder than he had realized. So hard, in fact, that he began to wonder if the price had been worth all the pain and hardship he'd endured. Losing his partner and friend, Jack Cross, had made it all that much harder to deal with.

The only friends he had could be counted on the fingers of one hand, and each and every one of them was in the business too.

As the plane winged its way toward its destination, he began to regard his future with SI6 with trepidation.

Had it all been worthwhile?

———

Niall had watched the safe house from a distance. He had arrived to ensure he would already be in place before they arrived.

Just two minders, that had to mean the place must be brimming with a full security suite.

Security measures were a problem to be sure, but Frank had told him of jobs pulled off under similar circumstances with complete success.

The key to this would be speed. He'd have to do this as fast and as soon as possible. If they suspected trouble, then Goff's minders would assume whoever came at them wouldn't be familiar with the layout. They would not expect someone to know from the start where they were.

This was a huge advantage! He'd gladly use it.

Niall got out of his car and pulled the collar of his jacket high up around his neck and his baseball cap down low over his eyes, concealing as much of him as possible. Once he retrieved the padded blue bag from the rear seat, he turned and slowly walked up to the front door.

Keeping his head bent low, he rang the doorbell. The camera above the door made a whirring sound as it swiveled to get a better view of him. The angle of the cap and the fact he kept turning away made it impossible for anyone watching inside to make a positive ID.

A voice came over the intercom by the door, "What do you want?"

"Food delivery, mate," Niall replied in an impeccable cockney accent.

"We haven't ordered any food. You've been had. Now get lost," the voice replied angrily.

"Look, mate, I got the address right, and I've got your food here, so come the fuck down here and pay for it," Niall argued.

"I won't tell you again, we haven't ordered anything. Now go away before I call the police," the voice said again, this time forcefully.

"Hold on, let me check," Niall said as he made a show of checking the receipt. "Sorry mate, you're right. You didn't make the order, it was made for you, don't know who by, just got a number."

"What's the number?" another voice asked.

Niall read out the number of Special Branch HQ.

The second voice said, "Wait there, I'll be right down," then, without turning the intercom off, Niall heard him say, "The boys at HQ must've sent provisions."

Niall readied himself for the attack; he turned away from the camera, pretending to put the receipt away, and reached for a Walther PPK with a Carswell silencer attached.

When the door opened, he turned to face the man standing in the doorway. The man's eyes went wide as he spotted the Walther in Niall's hand; the realization of what was about to happen registered on his face just as the hole between his eyes appeared and blood trickled down his nose. Blood and gore from the gaping hole in the back of his head painted the wall behind him. The man's body went limp, crumpling to the floor like a rag doll.

Niall was already walking past the dead body before the other guard had time to register what had happened. When the other guard came to see what was going on, Niall double-tapped the trigger and dropped him where he stood.

Goff came through from the kitchen at the back, asking, "Is there anything to eat in this dump?"

When he saw Niall standing over Trent's dead body

and Walker's lying in the hallway, all thoughts of food quickly evaporated.

"Frank says hi," Niall said coldly as he shot him in the head.

Slowly he walked over to Goff, bending to check for a pulse. There was none.

CHAPTER NINE

Mike found traveling somewhere and not having to plan for a mission was a refreshing change.

The heat was at its height at just after half two in the afternoon, it had hit him full force the moment he set foot off the plane an hour earlier. Now, as he wondered if there would be anyone to greet him, he realized the details Tony had supplied were scarce, to say the least.

As he walked out into the blazing sunshine of a pure azure sky with his bag in hand, he saw a young man walking towards him. He had wavy hair the color of ebony and an uncertain smile below deep brown eyes.

"Good afternoon, Mister Flynn?" he greeted, his voice soft and smooth.

"Who's asking?" Mike said coolly, his senses on sudden alert. As he was on leave, he had considered leaving his gun at home but opted instead to bring it, and as regulations stipulate, agents of SI6 are supposed to carry a weapon at all times. In this regard, and due to regulations, his Beretta was locked and sealed in his luggage. There was no way to get to it in time if this person was a threat.

"I'm Nicos, Mister Flynn. I've come to take you to the villa. Georgios will see you later; he's busy at the moment at the restaurant. Mister Tony called and arranged it all, sir," replied the young man now with a radiant smile.

"Mister Tony, Tony Armstrong?" Mike asked.

"Yes sir, he is our very good friend," Nicos replied amiably.

"There's no reason to keep calling me 'sir', Mike will do just fine."

"And you can call me Nicos, sir, sorry," Nicos said, then slapped his thigh as if punishing himself for his error. "Now let us go, please. I am to go to the restaurant, my shift starts soon."

"I'm all yours," Mike said as he followed Nicos to the parking lot where a battered old Ford pickup truck sat waiting for them. Before long, they were on their way to Stalis, Nicos driving the truck expertly along the narrow roads. They chatted about general matters to fill the time. Mike learned that Nicos had worked for Georgios for over seven years, even though he was still only twenty-three. He had met Tony some years ago when he had helped Georgios out with a private matter, the details of which he was reluctant to go into any further. Ever since then, they had been in his debt and had considered him a close personal friend of the family.

In turn, Nicos learned that Mike worked for Tony and was there on holiday.

The ride lasted close to two hours, with the last quarter taken up with Nicos having to concentrate as he negotiated some very narrow, twisting roads that climbed into the hills overlooking the familiar stretch of coastline that most tourists associated with Crete.

A white stone villa came into sight as they approached, it had three floors, and God only knew how many rooms. The side facing the coast had floor-to-ceiling glass doors that opened out onto a balcony that he was sure provided a spectacular view. In fact, every room on the top two floors had a balcony large enough to accommodate a good-sized table and chairs.

The roof had a straw-covered awning that served as a veranda, and as they drew nearer, Mike could make out a good-sized barbeque sitting in one corner, just waiting to be called into service.

At the front of the property was a large swimming pool, the azure blue clear water that hardly rippled was an absolute dream on a day like today.

Striking out for the edge with a languid backstroke was an absolute vision gliding along almost as if the water was caressing her lithe young body.

Reaching the side of the pool, she pulled herself clear of the water with practiced ease. As she straightened, the woman quickly wiped the water from her eyes and then her forehead with a graceful movement of her hands. She stood at five feet seven, the tiny bikini she wore complimented her athletic figure. The water droplets glistened on her tanned body as she watched them approach.

Her dark hair was pulled back into a tight ponytail that hung almost down to her backside. Her full and sensual lips parted into a welcoming smile as she saw them. Her deep brown eyes sparkled, adding to her joy when she recognized who it was.

She waved her arms, shouting, "Nicos, Nicos, you're back."

"Who's that?" Mike asked.

"Maria, Georgios' daughter, she's like my sister," Nicos replied.

From the way Nicos looked at her, Mike figured he wished they were more. He couldn't blame him though, she was gorgeous.

Nicos stopped the truck in front of the villa and killed the engine. Maria came running as they got out and threw her arms around Nicos' neck, giving him a big hug.

"You're back," she said, then glancing at Mike, asked, "This him?"

"This is Mister Flynn," he said as she let go of him. She stood, scrutinizing Mike with a curiosity that was slightly unnerving.

"Call me Mike," he said smiling.

"Come, I'll show you to your room," she said.

"I'll see you both later at the restaurant," Nicos said as he turned to leave.

Maria waved goodbye as Nicos got back in the truck, then suddenly turned on her heels and began walking off towards the villa. Mike quickly grabbed his luggage and fell in behind her, trying not to stare at her behind as she sashayed her way into the villa.

His room was on the top floor, small but functional. There was a good-sized bed, a wardrobe, a dressing table, and in the adjoining shower cubicle was the toilet and washbasin. Everything he could possibly need.

"I'll let you settle in. If you want anything, I'll be downstairs in the pool," she told him with a smile as she left him alone to unpack.

Even though she had left the room, her presence remained.

This holiday was shaping up nicely, he thought.

He quickly unpacked, a habit born of years of experience, not that he'd brought that much with him anyway. Experience had taught him to travel light. He threw off his clothes, pulled on a pair of swim shorts, and went downstairs, diving into the pool as soon as he got there. The cold water was a welcome shock after the warmth of the afternoon sun. After a few lengths of the pool, he felt himself begin to relax, the tension in his body easing away a little more. He was used to living at a constant heightened level of awareness, his job demanded it of him, but it was almost impossible to switch off at times like these. Some agents and soldiers had cracked under the strain and pressure he lived under. He still wondered, was all this worth it?

"Are you hungry?" Maria's voice snapped him back to the here and now, reminding him of how hungry he was.

"Yes, starving, actually. I haven't eaten since last night. I fell asleep on the plane, so I missed out on the food," he replied, realizing he was probably saying too much. He wasn't normally that forthcoming with anyone he had just met.

"So let's go to my father's restaurant, he's expecting us. You can sample our food there," she suggested.

"Sounds like a great idea," he said.

"I'll just go get dried off and put some fresh clothes on and meet you down here in a few minutes," he said, grabbing a towel as he headed upstairs to his room. Mike quickly showered and dressed in a pair of tan chino shorts, a cool white cotton tee shirt, and a pair of Gola sandals. Without even thinking, he assembled his Beretta and tucked it into the waistband at the small of his back under his shirt. It was just another habit born of his years living on the edge.

Comfortable with his preparations, he returned downstairs once more to the pool area to find Maria already waiting for him. She, too, had changed and was wearing a pair of dark blue shorts and a white blouse that gaped open at the neck, showing quite a bit of cleavage. She also sported a pair of sandals on her feet, he noticed them as his eyes traveled up her smooth and tanned legs before noticing the motorbike she sat astride.

"Ready when you are," he said, snapping back to attention.

"Climb on behind and hold on tight," she told him with a mischievous smile.

"Okay," he agreed as he swung his leg over the rear seat and grasped her waist.

She gunned the engine and set off down the driveway towards the open road, such as it was.

The wind buffeted them as she picked up speed, and he found he had to lean forward into her to keep from falling off, an excuse to get closer to her he gladly took advantage of.

The journey into Stalis, or Stalida as the Cretans knew it, only took twenty minutes or so. Upon arrival, she drove around the back of her father's restaurant and parked her bike by the rear kitchen door entrance.

The moment they set foot through the door, they heard voices, loud voices, angry voices that stopped them in their tracks.

Georgios was a big man, almost six feet tall, but his broad shoulders and thick arms made him look enormous. The three men with him were all as tall as he was, dressed in slacks and cotton shirts open down to the waist. Georgios was dressed for work, black trousers, and a white shirt with only the top two buttons undone.

He was facing a man while the other two stood at his shoulders slightly behind, ready to attack at any moment without him being aware. It was a tough situation, but

Mike got the impression that Georgios could handle himself quite sufficiently.

They were arguing, but the moment they saw Mike and Maria enter, everything stopped.

"Father, are you alright?" she asked, her voice full of concern.

Georgios turned at the sound of her voice. Mike saw the look on his face, the look of someone caught in a lie. In an instant, it was gone, replaced by a beaming smile for his daughter.

"Yes, my dear, I'm fine. These three are just leaving," he said, his voice deep and resonant.

The man in front of Georgios looked at him, his eyes like thunder. "We'll go when this is finished and not before."

Mike stepped past Maria towards the group. "I think you'll find, gentlemen, that whatever this is, it's finished, like the man says."

"And just what makes you think that's right, my friend? Before you answer that, just consider what this is that you're sticking your nose into. You could end up hurt, hurt really bad," replied the spokesman for the three men.

"Your accent, Russian is it? Let me guess, Mafia. You are trying to extort funds from my friend here who refuses to play along? How am I doing?" Mike said coolly.

"Very good, seems like your friend here has been around a little, knows a thing or two," the Russian said to Georgios. Then turning his cold stare toward Mike, he said, "But if I were you, I would try to persuade him to mind his own business and not get involved. One more life at risk is probably more than your conscience will allow."

"I can speak for myself, and I make my own decisions,

but thank you for your concern. You see, these people are friends of a friend of mine, which makes them my friends too. Where I come from, we stick by our friends. So to make it perfectly clear, you had better leave now before things start to get ugly," Mike said. He glanced at one of the other goons and said, "Oh, too late."

Ready to fight, the two men stepped forward, but Georgios blocked them by holding his arms out. "Not in here, not now," he said in a voice like iron.

"Again you try to order us around, Georgios, this has got to stop. It is us who are in control here, not you. It is time you learned the truth of this," said the leader as he drew a butterfly knife, expertly flipping it open.

Mike stepped forward quickly, bringing his right hand down on the man's wrist with enough force to make him drop the knife and quickly elbowed him straight in the face with the same arm, snapping his head back in a splatter of blood and broken teeth. The man staggered across the kitchen as the other two eagerly joined in. As they stepped up, Mike kicked the first one in the gut with his right foot doubling him up, then pivoted, smashing a tremendous left cross into the side of the other man's face.

Georgios brought his knee up into the first man's face as he staggered by, sending him crashing to the floor.

Mike turned just in time to see the leader pick up his knife and come lunging across the kitchen at him. Stepping into the low attack, he blocked the arm holding the knife by crossing his hands at the wrists to catch the attacker's arm. Mike twisted the arm into a full arm bar, his arm locked straight and forced up against the joint. The man screamed in pain as the ligaments in his shoulder threatened to give way and he dropped the knife. Mike smashed his right palm heel down onto the upturned elbow joint, smashing it with an audible crack that made Maria shudder.

"Now leave while you still can, and don't come back. Next time you won't get off so lightly. Put this down to me being hungry. I won't be so generous next time," Mike said. His voice was hard and cold, devoid of emotion. By the look on the others' faces, Mike knew his message had been delivered.

The three goons gathered themselves up and scuttled out the rear door the way Mike and Maria had entered earlier.

"I thank you, my friend," Georgios said, but Mike saw something in his eyes that told another story. Cretans, like Greeks, are proud people; this incident had brought shame on him. It was an embarrassment to him, not being able to handle his own affairs in front of guests.

Georgios looked at Maria and shrugged his shoulders. She bowed her head and said, "I know you said no, Father, but as you just saw, these men will not take no for an answer. You've worked too long and too hard to allow scum like this to take what is rightfully yours."

Complete understanding dawned at that moment. Mike knew then what he had walked into here was a setup, and Tony was the perpetrator.

"You had no idea I was coming, did you, sir? In fact, you forbade Maria bringing me here. She went against your wishes, I imagine?" he said, staring at the proud man.

Georgios said, "Yes, Maria was afraid for my safety, I suppose, even though I told her I could handle it. She suggested we ask Tony for help. I told her we could handle it ourselves."

"Don't be too hard on her; she was worried about you,

that's all. She obviously loves you very much and doesn't want to see you get hurt."

"I'm afraid now things will only get worse."

Mike understood exactly what he meant. He knew what the Mafia was like; they would have to retaliate for tonight's action. They couldn't allow anyone to learn of this rebellion.

He nodded his head in agreement.

"But they are gone, you sent them away, Mike," Maria said, smiling.

"It's not as simple as that. I know what these people are like; I've had dealings with them myself. They won't give up until they're made to," Mike said. Turning to Georgios, he offered, "I can help, sir, if you'll allow me to."

"Please, Father, Tony wouldn't send someone if he didn't think the threat was real. If he says they'll be back, we have to listen," Maria pleaded.

"Oh, they'll be back alright, my dear, and next time we won't be able to fend them off with just our bare hands," Georgios said.

He turned to Mike and said, "I don't have to like it, but I must agree with you. I will accept your offer of help," he continued, and he extended his hand to Mike.

Mike shook the offered hand and said, "Don't be too hard on her; she was worried about you, that's all."

"She's headstrong that one, just like her mother. Come, let's go through to the restaurant and get you something to eat. No one can say you haven't earned it tonight," he replied.

"Now you're talking my kind of language!"

CHAPTER TEN

Bainbridge was sitting in his office when the intercom beeped, interrupting him. Annoyed, he asked, "Yes, Jen, what is it?"

"Sir, there's a call for you, urgent. It's from Number Ten," the pleasant voice on the other end replied.

"Then you'd better put it through."

"Bainbridge here," he said, working to keep the annoyance from his voice.

It was Duncan Nesbit, the PM's private secretary. "The Prime Minister would like to see you right away, General. This matter is most urgent."

"I'll be right there," he replied, immediately ending the call and simultaneously pressing the button on the intercom. "Miss Austin, send a car around for me immediately, seems I'm needed at Number Ten. Hold all my calls until I return," he had a few minutes to finish up a few things he'd been working on while he waited for his car to arrive. Try as hard as he did though he could not concentrate knowing that he had been summoned. This usually spelled trouble. He couldn't help but wonder just what precisely had gone wrong.

———

In a short while, his car arrived and he was transported to the Prime Minister's residence, where he was shown straight through to the PM's private study.

The door opened, and he was led in. Seated behind a desk before him festooned with files piled high was the Prime Minister, Andrew Chambers.

He was still tall, youthful, and energetic; the only sign of the stress of his job showed in the slight greying at the temple of his jet-black hair.

The populace was accustomed to his ready smile that had charmed them into putting him through for his second term, that and his outstanding record in office. However, that smile was not evident today as Bainbridge entered the room.

"What a complete and utter balls up, General," Chambers said, annoyed, catching Bainbridge completely off-guard.

"I beg your pardon, sir?" Bainbridge asked, wondering what he'd walked into.

There was a second person in the room, seated before the desk, whom he had recognized the moment he set foot in the room.

Stuart Tyler, the Deputy Director of MI6 and the man who had asked for his assistance earlier.

He began to smell a rat.

"Oh, I don't mean you, General; I've just been informed of the release of Frank Grogan. It seems that the star witness we had concealed was killed early this morning, so the Special Branch informs me. This has not been released to the news media, as you must be aware if this ever got out, considering that the witness was actually on your payroll, Tyler, and obviously planning to sell secrets of national importance to a terrorist, it would be a disaster. I can hardly believe this is happening. A 'D' notice has been applied to prevent the media reporting on any of this. The reason I've called you here, General, is so you can hear for yourself what Stuart has just informed me of," Chambers said, handing over the floor to Tyler.

Tyler looked at Bainbridge and sombrely said, "Goff was killed by one of Grogan's men."

"How is that possible, unless there is a leak inside MI6, SI6, or Downing Street?" replied Bainbridge, his eyes going wide with disbelief.

"There isn't a leak," Tyler said confidently.

"How can you be so sure?" Bainbridge queried, his eyes boring into the other man.

"Because I know how the information got to them. You see, several months ago, we managed to place one of our own in Grogan's group."

"I don't see how that is even possible. They are notoriously good at rooting out operatives, that's why they've remained at large for so long."

Tyler leaned forward in his seat, clearly nervous about what he was about to divulge.

"Grogan's right-hand man, as you all know, is Niall Quinn. They grew up together, and he is extremely protective of him. He would never allow anyone to get near him, but recently someone did. Sean Rourke, he's a soldier with the SAS.

"He was born in Belfast, but his parents made him go live with his uncle in London when he was ten. His father made him promise he would never set foot in Ireland while he was alive, and he never did until six months ago, when he attended his father's funeral. Someone approached him from Grogan's gang, telling him the Army had killed his father as they were hunting one of the boys. Total hogwash, of course, but Rourke saw an opportunity to get inside their gang. He took it to his CO, who brought it to us. We, of course, agreed, and when he was next approached, he played along.

"Quinn never truly trusted Sean though, and was always trying to catch him out. It was Sean who warned us of the deal Goff was trying to make. I'm not sure what happened after that."

"What's that supposed to mean? Have you lost contact with him?" Bainbridge asked, fearing where this was going.

"In a way, yes. We sent out a recall command when Grogan was caught, but we've heard nothing. I'm thinking he gave them the location of the safe house Goff was being kept at. He'd have knowledge of it from his time in the SAS; we frequently use them for security. It would be his way of proving his loyalty, and there's only one reason he would do that."

"Which is?" Bainbridge already knew the answer, but he wanted to hear the words from Tyler's mouth.

"I think Sean's gone rogue."

Bainbridge turned away from Tyler, his teeth clenched as he thought of the ramifications. "Great, that's all we need. Not only is Grogan free again, but we also have an ex-SAS, ex-MI6 operative working with him. What else can go wrong?" he grated through his teeth, his fists balling in his lap.

Chambers looked at him, his brow creased with concern. "General, I'm tasking you and your unit to do whatever is required to resolve this matter. Use extreme force if necessary. Deputy Director Tyler will assist in any way he can, is that clear, Stuart?" he said in a tone that brooked no argument.

"Perfectly, Prime Minister," Tyler replied.

"There can be no jurisdictional disputes over this one, gentlemen. SI6 will take point on this, and MI6 will assist."

"Yes, sir," Bainbridge said before adding, "You have my word we will do our utmost to bring this to a speedy and successful conclusion."

"That's all I needed to hear, gentlemen," Chambers said. "I'm sure you want to get right on this, so I won't keep you any further," with a dismissive wave of his hand, the meeting was abruptly at an end.

The two men quietly rose and left the room. In the corridor outside, Bainbridge said, "Let me have the entire file on this op ASAP. If we want to salvage anything from this, we have to move fast."

CHAPTER ELEVEN

Sean Rourke was tall, standing just over six feet, with an athlete's build gained from his years of active service with the Regiment. His straw-colored hair was cut short, sitting atop a rugged face with high cheekbones inherited from his Gaelic forebears. Eyes the color of an Icelandic sky looked back at him in the rearview mirror of his Ford Mondeo as he answered his phone.

"They will be at the hotel shortly. You know what you have to do, no loose ends, is that clear?" The electronically altered voice said.

"Perfectly clear," Rourke replied as he stared at himself in the mirror, he felt no shame in what he was about to do. It was necessary, that's all.

"When it is done, keep your phone on and await new orders. You will sever all ties with MI6 and your old life. You now belong to the Hierarchy," the voice said, and the line went dead.

Rourke put away his phone and started the engine.

This was the first day of the rest of his life. His old

life was dead, as dead as Frank Grogan and Niall Quinn would very soon be too.

————

Bainbridge was seated at his desk when Tony came in.

"How was your meeting with the PM, sir?" Tony asked.

Bainbridge quickly told him everything he had learned at Number Ten about Rourke and Tyler's involvement.

"Do you believe it, sir?" asked Tony when he'd finished.

"Quite frankly, if Stuart Tyler told me today's date, I would still consult a calendar to make sure. This, I'm not sure of. It smacks of plausibility, but then most lies have a grain of truth running through them. If this is true, then we have our work cut out," Bainbridge told him candidly.

"Sir, I'm not sure what the PM wants of us on this. I mean, Grogan has been notoriously elusive in the past, and now he has a rogue agent on board. There's not going to be an awful lot we can do to catch him. After his narrow escape, he'll go to ground, and I doubt we'll even see his shadow let alone get close enough to nab the bastard," Tony said, stamping around the office in frustration.

"I take your point. We'll just have to hope we catch another break like we did last time, but I'm not holding my breath. You'd better prime Flynn; I have a feeling he's going to be needed again."

"Actually, sir, I sent him to Crete on some well-earned leave, he's staying with some friends of mine. I was contacted by their daughter, it seems he was being terrorized by some Russian Mafia thugs, so I sent Mike over on the pretense of him getting some rest. You know how it is with these types, after a few days of sunning himself, he'd be bored to death and looking to find some trouble. I just organized some for him."

"Right, but next time, clear it with me first, Colonel," he said. The use of his rank showed Tony he was annoyed he'd made his best operative unavailable.

"Copy that, sir."

"Give him a quick call, get a sit-rep, and if he's needed there a bit longer, check who we have on file we can pull back in."

"I'll get right on it, sir," Tony replied as he took out his phone to call Mike.

———

"Colonel, what can I do for you?" Mike asked.

"What's your situation there, Mike?"

"Well, sir, the accommodation is very nice, clean, and comfortable, and my hosts are very helpful and friendly, but that's not what you meant, is it?"

"No, I'm afraid it isn't. A situation has arisen back here, and I may have to recall you. What's your take on the problem there?"

"Well, the problem isn't so easy, sir. I have made contact with the main players and sent them on their way, but they'll be back. You know how the Russians play, sir. They'll have to send a message to everyone else. This may get dirty and very wet. How am I covered on the local end of things?"

"We have some people who can help in that area, at least with the clean-up, but as far as the rest, I'm afraid you're on your own."

"I should be used to that, sir," Mike said.

"You needed a change of scenery, and they needed someone who could help. Seemed like a good idea to combine the two at the time. How long before you can wrap things up?"

"Hard to say, sir. A lot will depend on the Russians and on how they respond to my intervention in this matter. I can't see them just leaving things as they are. There's no telling how long it'll be before they make their move though."

"You'll just have to prod them along then. Do whatever it takes to clear this up and get home, you're needed here. Grogan has been released, and there are complications," Tony finally said, dropping the bombshell.

Mike's eyebrows knitted together in a frown, and he balled his fist as the news sunk in.

"I'll do what I can, sir," he replied and put his phone away. Looking up, he saw Maria standing close by.

"Who was that?" she asked as she looked up into his troubled eyes.

"Tony," he said.

"Something's wrong, what is it?" she asked perceptively.

"There's a problem back home, and I may have to return sooner than I thought. So I need to make sure it's safe here for you and your father," he told her with a reassuring smile.

———

Tony put his phone away, returning to the General. "The situation there is not resolved, and he's reluctant to leave it that way. I sent him there, and he feels responsible for my friends because of his actions. I'm afraid we may have to count him out for at least a few days, sir."

"What about sending him some backup to help speed things along? See if you can get hold of Jack Cross," Bainbridge suggested.

Tony looked at the General, his eyebrows arching in surprise, "You do know Jack has retired from SI6?"

"Not in the slightest, he's just on extended leave. I can't afford to have one of my best operatives running around free out there, what if he decided to talk about what we do here? No, that was unthinkable, I knew he was having doubts about his role in SI6, and with having a young family, I just gave him time to spend with them. He'll soon realize where his place is, here in this unit. Besides, what else would a man like Jack Cross do in the real world?" Bainbridge explained.

"And what if he doesn't want to come back?"

"Tell him his best friend is in a tight spot and needs his help, and don't look at me like that, Tony. You know as well as I do that they've been keeping in touch since Jack thought he resigned. If that doesn't work, just explain that he's still working for SI6 and still bound by the Official Secrets Act, and refusal to cooperate is insubordination."

SI6 personnel were not supposed to fraternize with those outside the profession. Tony knew both Mike and Jack thought they had kept their regular meetings quiet, but he should have known the Old Man would find out somehow. The only thing keeping him from stopping their meetings was the fact that, strictly speaking, Jack was not an outsider, he still worked for him, and Bainbridge was using this to his advantage.

"I see, sir. I'll get in touch with him right away," he said as he regained some of his composure.

"Don't feel bad about this, Tony. I've known from the start about them keeping in touch. You may not think this, but I try to keep everyone's best interests at heart. What we do is at the extreme end of things, and for us, all of us, to perform at our best, it's vital we have a nurturing environment."

"What happens when one of us wants to leave and pursue a life outside of SI6, sir?" Tony asked, dreading the answer.

"There is no life outside of SI6, Tony, you know that. Once you join, you're in for life. You could never adapt to a normal life after doing what we do," Bainbridge told him.

"What happens if they don't see it like that, what about Jack? He thinks he's already out?"

"Then he has to be told the truth."

Tony went to say something but thought better of it. Jack Cross was a friend of his too, and what the General was suggesting felt like betrayal to him.

"Bainbridge saw the anguish in his Chief of Staff's eyes and said, "Don't worry, Tony, if it needs to be done, I'll do it. I make the big decisions here; that's why I'm in charge."

"That's not necessary, sir. I'll go talk to him person-ally, now," he said then turned and left the room.

CHAPTER TWELVE

Tony left HQ in a staff car, a Bentley Mulsanne, and headed for the Cross family home in Vauxhall.

When the contact he'd been looking for popped up on his phone, he paused a moment, briefly thinking about what he was about to do before finally pressing the call button; when a man's voice answered, he said, "Jack, this is Tony."

"What can I do for you, Colonel?" Jack answered guardedly.

"Just called ahead to ensure you're at home. Stay where you are. I'll be there to brief you in a few minutes." Then, before Jack could say a word, he hung up, ending the call.

He sat back in the comfortable leather seats of the car and thought again about what he had to do.

———

"What does Tony want?" Melissa Cross asked expectantly. She had heard her husband answer his phone and stood next to him.

Jack looked at her, the concern evident on her face in the lines creasing her forehead.

"I don't know," he said, hoping to placate her.

"He's never paid us a visit before, has he," she said, her hands on her hips.

"No, but—"

"But what, Jack? What possible reason can he have for visiting us other than what we both already know?" He watched as she stormed away from him.

Jack hung his head, he knew she was right. Tony had never visited them, ever. He was their friend, but he'd always kept a professional distance from them, allowing them to have some semblance of normalcy in their lives.

This could only mean one thing. He wanted him to return to the unit.

"I guess we'll know pretty soon then," he said, but he knew it was a lame response. As far as he was aware, he was retired from SI6, although no official paperwork had ever been handed in. He thought a verbal resignation had been enough considering the covert nature of what SI6 did; it seems he may have been wrong.

After a few moments, Melissa returned to him, her big brown eyes brimming with tears. "What're you going to do?"

"If I have to, I'll resign my commission and leave the Army," he said.

"If you have to, I thought you'd decided you couldn't do this anymore? I don't know what you do, but you said you couldn't put us through this any longer. Now it's 'if you have to'? What's changed, Jack?" she asked emphatically as she leaned with one hand on a worktop while the other cradled the slight bump in her belly.

Jack looked away, regretting his choice of words

instantly. As soon as the words left his mouth, he knew she'd seize on his Freudian slip and batter him with it. If the truth be told, he was missing the action, but he could never tell her that. His last mission with Mike that had gone tits up; it was then that he came to the decision that he couldn't leave this world knowing his wife and daughter would have to struggle without him. He couldn't live with the knowledge that he may not be around to see their daughter grow up. Now though, after spending a few months on leave, he was getting a severe case of cabin fever. All his fears for his family had faded into the dark recesses of his mind as he tried to come up with any excuse to return to work.

"Nothing's changed, babe," he lied.

"Well, you'd better be more convincing than that when Tony gets here because that lie is written all over your face."

Before she could continue, there was a knock at the front door.

Jack gently squeezed her shoulder as he went to open the door to his old boss.

"Good to see you, Jack. You're looking fit and well," Tony said as he walked through the open door. The hand he'd held out in greeting was ignored.

"Before we begin, Colonel, can I just say that this is a wasted journey. I've resigned from SI6 and that's that," Jack said as he turned and walked down the hallway toward the kitchen.

Melissa came to stand by Jack supportively in the hope it would help him decide in their favor.

"Afternoon, Colonel. Can I get you anything?" she asked with a forced smile.

"No thanks, I'm good," Tony replied, his eyes straying

to her expanded belly; his coming here would be tougher than he realized, for all of them.

"Colonel, I would like you to be one of the first to know that we're going to have another child. That in itself should tell you that I can no longer work for you. I intend to resign my commission with the Army and find a job out in the real world," Jack said, looking Tony unwaveringly in the eye. He felt Melissa's small hand snake its way around his waist and knew she was firmly on his side.

Tony looked at them both, obviously, there was something troubling him. Jack could sense bad news was coming; he could see it clearly on the Colonel's face even though Tony prided himself on his self-perceived ability to remain poker-faced at times like these.

"I'm afraid that's not going to happen, Jack, not for the time being, at least," Tony said.

"What do you mean?" Melissa asked as she unwrapped her arm from Jack's waist to stand fierce in front of Tony like a lioness guarding her cubs.

"The General let you have extended leave which he's now rescinding. We need you to go to Crete and act as Mike's backup. We need him to finish up something out there and get back here as soon as possible. A situation has developed that needs our immediate attention. You'll get a full briefing when you get to HQ. This is not a request, Jack, this is a direct order. I'll expect you at HQ in an hour. I'll see myself out," Tony said, then turned and walked back to the door. As he opened it, he said, "Get your resignation in first thing to your regiment, and I'll see what I can do about getting you released, but this, today, this is happening, Jack."

The Colonel left, leaving them to stare at the door as he closed it behind him.

CHAPTER THIRTEEN

Sean Rourke had arrived early at the hotel Grogan and Quinn had been using and sat waiting for them on the street to show up.

The hotel was a rundown affair, the type frequented by prostitutes and drug dealers, and had been chosen for that very same reason. Grogan had deduced no one would be looking for them there.

Rourke saw the blue Mondeo turn in and drive down to the parking garage beneath the hotel. He knew they would use the stairs to walk up to the lobby to collect their room keys, so he waited.

He took out his pistol, a Walther PPS, and checked the load, ensuring he was carrying a full mag of eight rounds before he rammed the clip back in, racked the slide to inject a round into the chamber, then put the safety on. Placing the pistol back in the holster, he opened the door and got out of his car to stroll across the street.

A quick glance around told him all he needed to know as he entered the lobby. There was a desk in front of him, behind which sat a man with lanky hair that looked like it hadn't been washed in a week, reading something out of view. The desk clerk only gave Rourke a cursory glance as he approached.

No one else was in the lobby, and there were no CCTV cameras.

As he reached the desk, he pulled out his Walther, quickly attached a suppressor, and aimed straight at the clerk's head.

"Two Irish guys. What rooms?" he said in a cold, deadly voice that chilled the clerk. As the clerk's eyes strayed up to see the gun aimed at his head, he began to shake.

"You mean the two who just came in here?" he asked, his voice quivering with fear.

"Yes, what room numbers?" Rourke asked again.

"Thirty-two and three, third floor. Look, I don't want no trouble, man."

"Give me the master key," Rourke ordered.

The clerk reached behind him without taking his eyes off the muzzle pointed at his head and passed over the key. It was an old-fashioned type that fitted a mechanical lock; this wasn't the sort of hotel that had electronic locks.

"Don't worry, there'll be no trouble," Rourke said as he took the key then squeezed the trigger. The Walther's cough barely made a sound as the bullet smashed through the man's skull, painting the wall behind him with his blood. The clerk fell against the wall, twitched for a few seconds, then lay still.

"You just stay there, I won't be long," Rourke said to the corpse as he walked off towards the stairs.

He reached the third floor quickly, taking the stairs two at a time. Carefully, he opened the door, keeping the pistol down by the side of his leg, out of sight. Seeing no one was about, he made a note of the nearest door number and headed towards number thirty-two.

Traffic in the hotel would start to pick up later in the afternoon as the working girls went out to work the streets, but at this time of the day, it was quiet.

Two distinct voices could be heard as he approached the door. He placed the master key in the lock as quietly as he could, hoping they hadn't left their key in the lock. Feeling no resistance, he slowly turned the doorknob.

Without warning, he opened the door bringing up his Walther to aim for the first sound.

As the door swung wide, Grogan and Quinn both turned their heads at the sound of the door opening, Grogan on his right, Quinn to his left. Rourke fired, killing each with cold efficiency.

The Walther made a slight sound on each shot—four phuts, four shots. Each double-tap struck their intended target smack in the middle of the forehead.

Grogan was first, then Quinn. Blood splattered the walls as the bullets struck, snapping their heads back as the bodies tumbled to the floor.

Rourke took a moment to admire his handiwork while ensuring they were both dead. Once satisfied, he quietly left the room, locking the door behind him, secure in the knowledge it would be a while before the bodies would be discovered. Hotels like this did not have a maid service. *"It could be days before they were noticed,"* he thought as he wiped down the master key for prints.

———

A few moments later, Rourke was back in his car, reaching into his glove box for his coded mobile, and dialed a number.

"It's done," he said when the call was answered.

"Copy that, return to your room, and await further instructions," the voice of his contact in the Hierarchy said before ending the call abruptly.

Rourke put away his phone, started his car, and drove off.

CHAPTER FOURTEEN

Jack Cross arrived at the Headquarters of SI6, where he parked his car in the parking lot beneath, somewhat surprised to see his spot was still available, until he remembered what Tony had said about the General putting him on extended leave. Then it all made sense.

He entered the outer office where Jen was and saw her look up, a warm smile spreading across her lovely features when she saw him.

"Hi, Jack, how has your leave been going?" she said, as professional as always.

"You too, huh? How come I was the only one who didn't know I was on leave?" he replied.

"He's expecting you, you're to go right in," she said, neatly side-stepping his question.

"You'd better have this," he said, handing her the envelope he'd brought with him.

She took it from him. Her eyes lingered on it, then up to his face. "Is this what I think it is?" she asked, placing it down before her.

"My resignation, I'm making it official," he explained.

"I'll look after it for you. Go right in, he's waiting," she said, returning to her work on the computer screen before her.

As he opened the door, she glanced at his back as if ready to say something but thought better of it and returned her attention to her work.

"Good afternoon, sir," Jack said as he entered the large office.

"Good afternoon, Cross. We haven't a great deal of time on this, so I'll get right to the point," Bainbridge said by way of greeting.

"I'm fine, thanks," Jack said dryly, looking straight ahead.

"Quite," Bainbridge replied, ignoring the remark. He continued, "We had a tipoff about Grogan, which I sent Flynn to follow up on. A hacker working for MI6 offered him a NOC list. Deputy Director Tyler got wind of it and set up a meeting whereby we managed to grab Grogan and the hacker, Goff.

"Earlier, the hacker was targeted at the safe house and killed, we think by a member of Grogan's team. We now know the leak came from an MI6 agent ensconced within Grogan's team, a man named Sean Rourke. Up until recently, he was an SAS Captain seconded to MI6. We now think he has gone rogue and is working for Grogan.

"Needless to say, Grogan has been released, and we need Flynn back here to help with the investigation. I want you to go to Crete to help Flynn with his present mission so he can return here asap to join the investigation.

"The Gulfstream is standing by take you to Heraklion airport as soon as the Armourer has fitted you out with your equipment.

"Any questions?"

Jack looked down into the eyes of the General unable to keep the interest out of his own.

"What's Mike's present op, sir?" he asked, all anger at being called back to duty fading fast under the prospect of getting back to work.

"Colonel Armstrong sent him to help out a friend of his who was being bullied by the Russian Mafia. It turns out the situation is more dire than Tony suspected, that's why we need you there to help out. This is beyond our purview normally, but seeing as how it's the Russian Mafia, I thought it best to let this one ride. I have no desire to see that nasty group getting a foothold in any further territories in the West."

"I see, sir. Is that all?"

"Yes, see Major Bacon right away before catching your flight. Oh, and Cross, nice to have you back," Bainbridge said.

"I'm not back for long, sir; just until this op is done, then I'm gone. I've tendered my resignation, effective immediately," Jack said coldly, his anger returning as he realized what stung the most was that he'd been played.

Bainbridge looked up at him, and his face went blank, no expression, which threw Jack off a little. He'd seen that expression before; this was not good.

"We'll see," was all he said.

CHAPTER FIFTEEN

The Major was waiting when Jack reached the basement.

"Welcome back, Jack. You're looking fit and well," Bacon said with a smile.

"I'm not back, sir, well, not for long anyhow," Jack replied.

"Pity that. How was your leave?"

"What the fuck. Who doesn't know I was on leave?" he blurted out, immediately regretting his words. Major Bacon was a superior officer; his profanity could land him on charges.

"Don't be such an arsehole, Jack. You love this job, and you know it," Bacon chided him.

"You're right. I do love it, but it's time I left and put my family as my priority for a change instead of a country of faceless people who have no idea of the sacrifices we make for them. People who don't even know we exist," Jack snapped back.

"So you crave some recognition for what we do, is that it?"

"No, sir, you know that's not it."

"Then what is it, Jack? Tell me."

"I can't keep putting Melissa through the pain and worry of not knowing if I'll come home after an op. She deserves more than that."

"Every soldier, every policeman, fireman, and covert operative who has a family goes through the same debate with themselves. They go through the same heartache knowing the same thing, and they do it because they have to. If they didn't, then who else would? There are some people in the world who are gifted enough to tackle those tasks that the general population would rather not sully their hands on. They, my son, are called soldiers, and you are one of the finest I've ever seen. If you chose to do anything else, it would be a monumental waste of your talents."

"And what if I decide not to do this anymore?"

"Oh, you'll do it."

"How can you be so sure?"

"Isn't it obvious? Why else would you be here?"

Jack was unable to halt the brief smile that flashed across his face. He realized the Major was right. If he hadn't wanted to do this, he would have said to hell with it, remained at home, and faced the consequences. He didn't though he was here and, despite all his anger at being played, was looking forward to the challenge facing him.

"You could be right, to a point. Anyway, we'd better get going," he said, trying not to smile.

"Okay, well, your usual choice of weapon is a Browning, but let's see how you like this new Walther CCP. It stands for Concealed Carry Pistol and is designed just for that. It's smaller than the P99 but just as good. It's chambered for the 9x19 round and holds eight. It's ideal for a concealed weapon, and with that round, it'll have sufficient stopping power. Here, try it out," Bacon said, handing him the stripped-down weapon.

Jack inserted the clip into the butt, jacked the slide, and flipped the safety off. Placing ear guards over his head, he sighted down the range at a target, quickly firing off three rounds, followed by another grouping of three, followed by the last two in the clip.

Bacon inspected the target and noticed that the first three had struck the head just above the eyes in a tight grouping. The second salvo of three had hit center mass, while the last two had struck the heart almost as one hole.

Bacon turned to him and said, "Nice to see you've lost none of your edge."

"If that's all, Major, I'd better be off, bad guys to catch and all that, you know," Jack said as he took off the ear guards. He ejected the spent clip, chose a fresh one, and inserted it into the butt. On his way out, he grabbed three spare clips and a shoulder rig from the racks on the wall near the door and was gone.

CHAPTER SIXTEEN

Fairfax Airfield was a private flying club owned by SI6.

The Gulfstream 550 was parked on the tarmac, ready to go, with the passenger door opened as the crew waited for his arrival.

Standing in the doorway, he saw a young woman dressed in the club's uniform of light blue jacket and skirt. She smiled warmly when she saw him walk towards her.

"Good afternoon, sir. We'll be departing as soon as you're safely aboard. Captain Philips has logged in the flight plan, and we have a green light to depart when we are ready," she informed him as he walked up the stairs.

"Thanks," he replied with a smile. He took in the plush interior as he entered the spacious cabin and placed his go-bag in one of the overhead lockers before taking a seat. *"What other job could I get that incorporated first-class travel of this caliber?"* he thought.

"Can I get you anything before we take off, a drink maybe?" she asked, suddenly jolting him out of his thoughts as he realized she was standing at his shoulder.

He had been so wrapped up in his surroundings he hadn't noticed her following him to his seat.

He looked up at her and smiled, "Yes, please, a Scotch on the rocks if you have it?" he replied.

"Will Macallan do?" she asked.

Jack smiled and nodded, "That'll do fine, thanks. What's your name, Miss?"

"Flight Officer Warren, sir. I'll be your flight attendant during this flight as well as the return. The cabin crew is Captain Hankins and Lieutenant Middenhall, sir. I'll get you your drink," she said, leaving him to settle in.

When his drink arrived, he sipped the amber liquid allowing it to remain on his tongue as he tasted the smoky flavor. He swallowed and closed his eyes as the warming sensation spread through him. He leaned his head back against the seat and closed his eyes as he thought about what he had to do and what his future would bring.

———

Rourke picked his phone up at the first ring.

"Yes," he said calmly. He had been patiently waiting for new instructions and had wondered if they would come at all. Maybe he had been left out to dry, a sacrifice for the deaths of Grogan and Quinn.

"Deputy Director Stuart Tyler has a daughter, Mary. You are to capture her and take her to some remote location where her body will not be found straight away. Her death is to be a reminder to her father that we are not to be trifled with, is that understood?" the voice on the phone said.

"Perfectly," Rourke replied.

"Everything you need to know is being sent to your

phone as we speak. Read it and continue as instructed. Call me the moment you have her," and with that, the line was cut, leaving Rourke staring at his phone.

"Okay, Mary, let's see what you look like," he muttered as he quickly scanned through the pictures of the young woman that had been sent.

Mary Tyler was an attractive young woman with shoulder-length auburn hair and dark brown eyes. The pictures showed her in various outfits and different locations; after he'd viewed them all, he read through the text of her bio. She works for a finance company in the city and holds an associate position. She had not allowed her father's reputation or connections to influence her career, and judging by the limited contact she and her father had, Rourke wondered if the Hierarchy's plan would work. They were banking on familial ties being strong enough for this to work.

Putting his phone away, he left his hotel room. It was time to go to work.

———

Deputy Director Stuart Tyler was just preparing to leave his office when the phone rang.

Scooping up the handset, he said, "Yes."

His expression darkened as he listened to the report from the police liaison.

He placed the handset down, wondering what it all meant.

Frank Grogan and Niall Quinn had been found dead in a seedy hotel room earlier. No signs of a struggle, but all the earmarks of a professional hit were evident. None of this made any sense.

Picking up the handset once more, he dialed a secure number.

"Yes," Bainbridge said as the call was connected.

"Donald, I've just received a rather disturbing report from the police."

"In what regard, Stuart? You know as well as I do that in our business, any report can be disturbing, so you'll have to be more specific," Bainbridge responded.

"Grogan and Quinn have been found dead in a seedy hotel room here in London. You wouldn't have any knowledge of how that happened, would you?"

"What are you accusing me of, Stuart?" Bainbridge asked pointedly.

"I'm asking if you put out a termination order on them."

"The workings of this organization are of no concern to you, but in this instance, I can tell you that I did not."

"If you didn't, then who did?" Tyler mused.

"It is rather disturbing, seeing as how the two parties active in this situation had nothing to do with their deaths, it points to only one conclusion," Bainbridge observed.

"A third party was involved, but who? Who would want them dead?" Tyler asked.

"That, my friend, is the million-dollar question."

"Have you any ideas?"

Bainbridge thought for a few seconds. "Well, we know that Grogan was working for someone else. It's inconceivable to think he had the smarts to organize something like this on his own. We know Goff contacted him with an offer of selling the NOC list, so it's safe to assume he would have someone else in line for that. He would sell it to the highest bidder probably, unless he was working for someone else already."

"Yes, but who?"

"At the moment, your guess is as good as mine I'm afraid."

"I'll get my boys onto it right away and see if they can find any connection between Grogan and any other terrorist cells."

"I'll do the same. We still have Rourke to consider as well. It could've been him who made the hit."

"Why would he do that? He was working with Grogan. Why would he kill him?"

"We are assuming he was working with them and he's gone rogue. What if he was working as a double all along? What if this other group Grogan was working with recruited Rourke and ordered him to clear up all loose ends? It would make a twisted sort of sense."

"You're forgetting one vital detail. If this mysterious group wanted the NOC list, they have lost out, and now, if they've terminated their contract with Grogan, they can no longer acquire it."

"Think about it, Stuart. Once Grogan was captured, there was no way he was ever going to get them the list. This is their way of showing everyone working for them the price of failure."

"That makes sense, I suppose. Do you think it's over then? Do you think they'll try again but in a different way?"

"I have no idea, but I wouldn't take the possibility off the table just yet. All we can do is be extra vigilant."

"Okay, Donald, I'll get on to my people and see what they can come up with," Tyler said in closing before ending the call.

Tyler leaned back in his chair and breathed deeply. He had one last call to make then he was done. He had a feeling that this was far from over.

CHAPTER SEVENTEEN

Jack arrived at the US airbase on Crete without hindrance, thanks to an understanding and mutual respect between SI6 and the US government.

"Welcome to the NSA Souda Bay, sir. I've been ordered to give you this from your Armourer and assist you in any way I can," informed a young man dressed in a US Naval uniform.

"Thanks. Is there a car for me?" Jack asked as he took the kit bag from the ensign.

"It's right over there, sir," the ensign pointed to where the car was parked.

"Thanks, then that'll be all, I suppose."

Jack walked over to the car, placed his kit bag in the trunk then drove towards town to meet up with Mike.

The beachfront restaurant where Mike had eaten the night before was bustling when Jack arrived.

He saw Mike as he pulled up to the curb. He was talking to one of the waiters. Mike noticed him as soon as he drew up and came out to greet him.

Despite the situation, Jack could not help feeling pleased as he saw his friend pulling up to the curb.

"Jack, buddy, good to see you," Mike greeted.

Jack grabbed his offered hand, pulling his friend into a short hug.

"Man, it's good to see you," Mike said with genuine pleasure.

"Good to see you too," Jack replied as he quickly scanned their surroundings, checking out everyone present.

"Sorry you've been dragged into this, buddy, but it seems Bainbridge wants me back soon to handle the Grogan affair. Have you been briefed on that?" Mike asked in a low voice.

"Don't worry about it, Mike. I wouldn't be here if I didn't want to be, you know me."

"Really, what about Melissa, I thought—"

"You let me worry about her," Jack said, cutting Mike off. "Now, can you give me a sit-rep on what's happening here?"

Mike took a step back to look at his friend appraisingly.

"Don't give me that look, Mike. I'm only back for as long as it takes to finish this job. I miss this like you wouldn't believe, but my decision about my family still stands. I've handed my resignation in; this is the last job, not just for SI6 but for the Army too. Now can you give me a sit-rep so we can get this done, please?" he said, effectively shutting down any further comment.

Mike held up his hands in resignation, "Okay, buddy, if you're sure that's what you want. I did some digging into local affairs. My contacts said that the local Mafia bigwig is a guy named Grigori Petrov. That large *Petara* yacht you can see there in the harbor, that's his, and that's where we can find him."

"You're kidding me! That's your plan? You just want to sail right up to the largest yacht out there and persuade a Mafia leader to stop messing around with some friends of Tony's? Good plan, Mike."

Mike shrugged. "You say 'persuade', I say 'terminate'. What, you have a better idea?"

Frowning, Jack replied, "No, let's do this."

Smiling, Mike threw an arm around Jack's shoulders; "Man, I've missed having you around, buddy."

Their reunion was abruptly cut short by the sound of Jack's phone ringing. He reached for it noticing it was Bainbridge on the caller ID.

"Sir?" he said.

"Is Mike with you?" Bainbridge clipped.

"He's standing right here. What's up?" Jack asked, suspecting something had happened by the tone of his voice.

"Grogan and Quinn's bodies have been found in a hotel room here in London. From first reports, it looks like a professional hit."

"Well, that saves us a job then," Jack said.

"It also presents us with a problem."

"Yes, who was behind the hit, and will they stop there," Jack agreed.

"At the moment, the investigation is dead in the water. Stuart Tyler is looking into what might have happened, I'll see what we can do from our end, but it looks like whoever did this is tying up loose ends."

"What about Rourke, sir? If he's still out there, then he's still a threat."

"I'll have Mike look into that when he returns. Finish up there as soon as you can and get back here ASAP."

"Copy that, sir."

"I suppose you heard that," he said to Mike as he pocketed his phone.

Mike nodded, "Things are heating up back home. We'd better get this done with so you can get back to Melissa."

"Let's do this," Jack agreed.

———

Mary Tyler was walking towards her car in the car park below her office building when she heard footsteps approaching from behind.

She glanced quickly over her shoulder to see a tall, blond-haired man walking swiftly toward her.

"Can I help you with something?" she asked when she saw him smile disarmingly at her.

Before she could react, he thrust a pistol in her face.

"Yes, Miss Tyler, you can be very quiet and do as I say so I don't have to hurt you," the man said with calm authority. She nodded her head in agreement, terrified by the sudden sight of the pistol.

"Okay, that's good," the blond man said. "Right, we're going to get into your car and get out of here. Don't make any rash moves. I don't want to have to inform your father that you've been injured, or worse. Do everything I say, and this will all be over soon enough, and you can get back to your boring life."

"I've seen your face; I know enough to know my chances of getting out of this alive are slim. If you know *anything* about my father, then I suggest you leave now; this doesn't have to go any further. If you continue with this, my father will hunt you down and kill you," she said, clamping down hard on her fear, forcing herself to look him directly in the eye as she spoke.

"My word, you are a strong one, aren't you? Yes, I know about your father. I've worked for him in the very capacity you mention, you know, the hunting down and killing part, for quite some time. You're mistaken about living through this though. The reason you've seen my face is just to prove to dear old Daddy who has you, so you can testify to that. It also adds validity to what I tell him. He knows perfectly well what I'm capable of, he's ordered me to do far worse than what I'll do to you if he doesn't follow my orders." Rourke said.

Mary stared at him for a second, wondering what to do. Her bluff had been called; she had no cards to play.

"It doesn't mean I won't hurt you though, if you become a nuisance. Now let's go," Rourke ordered, gesturing with his pistol towards her car.

Reluctantly she acquiesced. Rourke watched as she entered the car on the passenger side, then climbed across to settle into the driver's seat with him following close behind. He ruthlessly shoved the pistol into her ribs, digging it in painfully.

"Just remember," he said, "you're going about your usual business, no false moves, no trying to get anyone else involved in this. No one has to die here, just play nice."

"Where to?" she asked, determined to show more confidence than she felt. She refused to show weakness to this man, whoever he was. She hadn't had a lot to do with her father of late; their differing opinions caused too much friction between them, but right now, all she wanted was for him to come and rescue her.

"Just drive, I'll give you directions," Rourke told her.

The car engine purred to life. She took a deep breath

and selected first gear, the tires squealed lightly on the concrete as she maneuvered the vehicle around corners and out of the car park. She really hoped she would get to see her father again, but a feeling of awful dread told her this would not end well.

CHAPTER EIGHTEEN

"Wow! She's a beauty," Jack commented as he caught sight of the yacht from the shoreline. He was looking through a pair of Steiner Navigator binoculars. They were at Agios Nikolaos, watching over Mirabello Bay, where the yacht was anchored. The expanse of crystal-clear water sparkled brightly in the sun.

"You can say that again, buddy. How do you want to do this?" Mike asked.

"Unless you want to swim out to it, we will have to find somewhere to hire or borrow a boat. Do you have anywhere in mind?" Jack asked as he continued to scan the yacht.

"Yes, there's a place nearby. I've already got one ordered. I suggest we wait until dark, then sneak aboard and have a look around, see what the situation is like there," Mike replied.

"I agree. It won't be long before the sun goes down, and then, wait. What's that?"

He had spotted something happening around the yacht.

"What is it?" asked Mike as he tried to see what had drawn his friend's attention.

"There's a small boat leaving the yacht. It looks like there are four men aboard, and they're heading towards the shore, right at us, in fact," Jack told him as he started to move.

"Do you think they've made us?"

"I'm not taking any chances. Let's move," Jack replied, and he walked back toward where the car was parked.

"You're carrying, I presume?" Mike asked.

Jack patted his side where his gun was holstered, "Yep, the US base made it much easier to bring my gun through customs," As they climbed into the car, Jack asked, "Where is this boatyard then?"

"Just a little way up the road. Let's wait a while first though. I want to see where those guys are headed."

They sat and watched the dinghy arrive. The four men transferred from the boat to a nearby car and drove off, heading towards Stalida.

Jack noticed Mike's expression alter, it was obvious something was bothering him, but the look on his face disappeared just as quickly as it first appeared. A fleeting thought perhaps, quickly discarded?

"We'll be able to make our move soon. Let's get the boat. By the time we have it, the sun will be down, and we can be gone before those guys return," Mike said.

———

Rourke directed Mary to an abandoned warehouse in Deptford.

There was a gaping hole in one of the walls where a

roller shutter used to seal the building when it had been in use. He instructed her to drive through it and stop.

"Where to now?" she asked, hoping they weren't going to stay there.

"We're here," he said, and she felt her heart sink.

He reached across her to turn the engine off, removing the key. "Get out; don't bother trying to run either. You don't want to get lost out here; it's not a nice neighborhood."

She did as instructed. Standing by the car, she looked around at the dismal surroundings. The light was fading fast, and her fear returned to take hold of her.

Pointing his gun at her, he said, "This way."

Rourke led her over to a hatch in the center of the floor in the largest area. Never taking his eyes off her, he reached down to pull the lid up, revealing a dark hole beneath.

"Down you go, girly," Rourke said with a hint of a smile.

Mary began to shake her head.

"You can either go in yourself, or I'll throw you in. Your choice, but make it fast," Rourke said impatiently.

"No!" she said, finding her voice at last, shaking her head vehemently.

Rourke sighed as he lowered his gun. He looked at her and, with a smile, asked, "Remember when I said you will live through this if you do what I tell you?"

Mary looked up at him tearing her eyes off the gaping hole in the floor, and nodded.

"I lied," Rourke brought up his gun, firing once. The bullet entered her forehead and smashed through the back of her skull, sending blood and bone fragments jetting out in a gory stream behind her as she fell backward. She was dead before she hit the floor.

Rourke strolled over to her inert form, grabbed one small foot, and dragged her over to the hatch, where he callously shoved her inside. Taking one last satisfied look at his work, he unceremoniously slammed the hatch shut, sealing her body inside. There was only one thing left to do.

He drove Mary's car to Heathrow Airport, handing it over to the Valet Parking attendants of Terminal Two. As the car was driven away, he walked away from the Terminal, intentionally losing himself in the crowd before hailing a taxi. He told the driver to drop him off at the nearest train station, where he entered the subway and joined the throng heading into town.

He was sure he had covered his tracks well enough. It would be a long time before they connected Mary's car at the airport with where her body was hidden. He honestly doubted they would ever find her.

As he sat back in his seat on the train, he took out a burner phone, it had been bought specifically for this job. There was just one number on it. Dialing the number, he listened as it rang. It was picked up almost immediately.

"It's done," was all he said.

He sat back and relaxed after pocketing the phone; he couldn't help but smile, congratulating himself on a job well done.

CHAPTER NINETEEN

Jack tossed the kit bag into the small boat Mike had hired, and the two of them pushed it down the ramp into the water.

The owner of the boat hire had looked at them with a strange expression when they had said they wanted the boat, specifically for tonight. His curiosity as to what they would be doing with his boat was readily apparent, but with a shrug of his shoulders and a forty percent increase in price, the owner had granted them their wish.

As they rowed out steadily towards the yacht, Mike asked, "What's in the bag?"

"Take a look; I'm not sure what's in there, to be honest. I was told it was from the Major. You know how he is, he hates for us to go into action unprepared," Jack replied as he continued rowing.

Mike opened the zip and peered inside. There were two Heckler and Koch MP5s, four blocks of C4, and an assortment of clips for the MP5s, Jack's Walther CCP and Mike's Beretta Cougar.

His eyes went wide like a kid opening presents on Christmas morning.

"Major Bacon sure knows how to keep a guy sweet," he said with a broad smile.

"What's the C4 for?" Jack wondered.

"Well we could blow some shit up," Mike replied with a wicked smile.

Jack nodded, "Sounds like a plan."

As they drew nearer to the yacht, the tension in the air ratcheted higher. Something felt off, completely wrong.

"Don't know about you, buddy, but I'm getting a bad feeling about this," Mike whispered.

The yacht was over a hundred and fifty feet in length and was the height of luxury for its class. Nevertheless, they could both feel something was wrong; there were no lights, and apart from the gleaming white superstructure glistening in the moonlight, there were no signs of life at all.

Quietly they allowed the dinghy to coast gently up to the side of the yacht, both men reaching out to buffer the approach and prevent them from bumping the hull of the larger vessel and unintentionally alerting anyone to their arrival should anyone be watching in the dark.

"Pass me one of those C4 bricks and a timer," Jack said.

Silently Mike passed what was needed, watching as his friend deftly attached it to the hull of the yacht and pressed a timer pencil into the brick of explosive. Slowly they circled the yacht, placing the remainder of the explosives around the waterline.

Once the last charge was in place, Mike motioned for Jack to steer their small craft toward the aft section to tie up. Once that was done, they checked their pistols and silently climbed aboard the sleek yacht.

Softly they made their way to the bridge, constantly listening for any sounds that would alert them to any presence on the seemingly abandoned vessel.

A light went on below the foredeck, illuminating a small portion of the boat. They instantly stopped, making eye contact, the same thought reflected on each of their faces, "*What the fuck!*"

Slowly they made their way to the foredeck. As they approached, a man sitting on a deckchair beneath a small awning looking out to sea came into view.

"Good evening, gentlemen. I wondered how long it would take you to find me," he said, his voice heavy with a thick Russian accent.

Mike and Jack froze in their tracks; as the man spoke, a group of armed men stepped from the shadows as if on cue.

"Come forward, let me see you," the man said.

Recognizing they were well outnumbered, Jack and Mike slowly raised their hands, offering no resistance as a couple of armed guards stepped forward to disarm them. Roughly they were prodded forward at gunpoint toward the stranger.

"Well, that could've gone better," Jack muttered.

"You must be the American who stuck his nose in my business the other day, and who's this?" the seated man asked, inclining his head toward Jack as they stood before him.

"You must be Grigori Petrov. I've heard a lot about you," Mike replied.

"That is correct, Mister Flynn. You still haven't introduced your friend here."

Jack shot off, "None of your damn business." The

man's cockiness was seriously grating on him. They'd obviously been set up; someone had to have known they were coming. Most likely, it's been someone Mike had been in contact with recently, perhaps friends of Tony Armstrong, he wasn't sure. But the simple fact that Petrov didn't know who Jack was showed how deep the mole was. It couldn't be someone at SI6, or Petrov would know his name. Mike had been the only one he was expecting.

"It really is of no interest to me who you are, I simply ask out of common courtesy. You will not live long enough to make a difference anyway," Petrov replied with a dismissive wave of his hand.

"You won't get away with this, you know, Petrov," Mike said calmly.

"Really, is that what you think? I'm afraid you are very much mistaken there. Let me ask you this, what precisely is it that you think I won't get away with?" Petrov replied with an unnerving self-confidence.

"This protection racket of yours, of course, we're here to put a stop to it," Mike said, matching the Russian's confidence.

"This I would like to see," Petrov said as he looked at his men guarding the two intruders and laughed.

"You have no idea even who I am, do you? You think I am a Russian Mafia leader, but I am not. Oh, I used to be, but now I work for a higher power."

"Don't tell me—God?" scoffed Jack, rolling his eyes.

Petrov's pleasant smile morphed into a deadly calm seriousness. "Have you ever heard of an organization called H.A.T.E.? No, of course, you haven't, no one has. It is an acronym for the Hierarchy for Anarchy, Terrorism, and Extortion. A little pedantic, I know, but you westerners have a childish fondness for your acronyms.

What is not childish is this organization. It has been hidden from the light for years. No one really knows how long it has existed, just that it does, and no one who crosses it lives...ever."

"If this thing is so damn secret, why the hell are you telling us about it?" Mike blasted back.

Jack chimed in, "Because he doesn't expect us to survive this encounter."

"Put them in the boat, take them out, and kill them. Do it silently and make sure their bodies are never found," Petrov ordered with a dismissive gesture.

Clearly, their conversation was at an end until a thought occurred to him. He turned to face them once more and said, "As to my little protection racket, as you call it, it will continue. You see, your little action the other day meant that I had to make a statement to *all my customers*, one they will never forget; it will ensure that they never again try to deny me what is mine."

"What did you do?" Mike asked, fearing the worst.

"He's going to kill your friends. That's his statement," Jack said.

"Oh, they're probably already dead. You must've seen the men I sent as you've been watching my yacht for quite some time," Petrov said, pausing to allow his words to sink in, his earlier smile returned when he saw the pain on Mike's face register.

Mike growled and lunged at the Russian, but a rifle butt to the ribs from one of the guards stopped him, dropping him to his knees.

"Take them away," Petrov commanded, turning his back on them. The audience was at an end.

CHAPTER TWENTY

Stuart Tyler reached for his phone as it rang; the screen read 'Unknown Number'.

"Yes?" he said, fear suddenly blooming inside him.

"If you do not follow my instructions, your daughter will die horribly," the cold voice on the other end replied dispassionately.

"Who is this?" Tyler demanded.

"It doesn't matter who this is, all that matters is that you do exactly as I say if you want to see your daughter again."

"How do I know you have her?" Tyler asked.

"You don't. All you need to know is she will die if you don't download the NOC list off your system and get it to me. You have one hour, then she dies."

Tyler shouted, "That's preposterous! Even if I could get it, there's no way I could get it downloaded and to you in that time frame."

"No, what's preposterous is that you thought you could meddle in our affairs without consequences," the voice said, abruptly cutting off Tyler's excuses.

"Who are you?" Tyler repeated.

"You can call me Mister Jones if that helps."

"Well, Mister Jones, I'm not doing anything until I get proof of life. I want proof my daughter is still alive," Tyler countered.

"Fine, I'll send you her pretty little right hand. You can run a DNA test from the blood you find on it to check it belongs to her, or maybe just run her fingerprints to see if she's on any database. Think you can do all that in one hour? Because if not, then I'll send you her head."

"You're bluffing," Tyler snapped.

"Okay, I'm bluffing. All you have to do is sit and wait for another fifty-nine minutes and thirty seconds to find out. First, I suggest you check out this little video clip I just sent to your phone."

Tyler pulled his phone from his ear to look at the screen. What he saw chilled his blood. CCTV footage from his daughter's car park showed Rourke approaching Mary and pointing a gun at her face before the two of them got in her car and drove off.

He knew the footage was genuine; there was no doubt about that. He and his daughter often didn't see eye to eye, but she had finally agreed on this one point, allowing him to use his influence to get hidden cameras installed overlooking her parking space just in case something should happen. He knew the man on the other end of the line was genuine too, seeing Sean Rourke's face gave horrible credence to his words, his threats were real.

Slowly he brought his phone back up to his ear, his mind in a tumult, desperately trying to come up with a plan.

"You have fifty-nine minutes; I'll call you back then."

The line went dead. His body sagged, heavy with fear and desperation, nearly bringing him to his knees.

His baby girl was in danger; he had to help her, no matter the cost.

He put his phone away, sat down in front of his computer, and booted it up. What was he going to do? He could not access the information for the NOC list directly, that would raise too many red flags. No, he would have to re-direct through various servers around the world, and that would take time. He glanced at the clock on his computer screen and did a quick calculation. It was going to be close.

———

Jack and Mike both dropped into a small boat that had been tied up around the front of the yacht after one of the guards had brought it around to the side on the Russian's order.

Jack kept his gaze fixed unerringly on the guard posted to watch them, the man kept a firm hold on his HK MP5 sub-machine gun. The last thing they wanted was a guard with an itchy trigger finger.

Jack noticed a bundle of chains with padlocks attached. The guard smiled cruelly as Jack glanced from him to the chains then back up to him.

It was obvious what was going to happen here. Gunshots in the bay would echo for miles, that would be too loud; instead, they planned on heading for deep water, where they would tie a length of heavy chain around them and deep-six them. It would be an agonizing death; the guard seemed to be looking forward to it.

He and Mike shifted to the far side of the boat as the other guard climbed aboard.

As they pushed off, Jack glanced at his wristwatch and

slid a sidelong glance at Mike. It would be tight, he just hoped their plan worked.

———

Petrov retrieved his mobile and quickly dialed the number for his superior.

It rang only once.

"It's done."

"Make sure you leave no loose ends," replied the voice on the other end.

"I have sent some of my men to—" the unfinished sentence hung in the air as, one by one, the C4 packs exploded beneath him, tearing the hull apart in massive fireballs that lit up the night sky.

———

The explosions distracted the guard's attention for a split second, but that was all Jack needed; he lunged for the man, knocking him off balance as he went for the sub-machine gun the guard held.

Maintaining his hold on the weapon with both his hands, Jack swung his right elbow up, smashing it hard into the startled face of the guard.

The man's head snapped to the side, enabling Jack to wrench the weapon free from his grip and turn it on the guard, immediately firing a short burst. The three steel-jacketed shells ripped through the guard's chest, forcing him backward and sending his body reeling over the edge of the boat into a cold black watery grave.

Jack pivoted around just in time to see Mike deliver a brutal punch to the other guard that landed hard in the middle of the man's face, forcing him to his knees; Mike reached forward to disarm the guard before delivering a retaliatory crushing blow to the man's head with the butt of the same gun he had used earlier aboard Petrov's yacht.

The man reared up to retaliate but was stopped short as Jack fired a short burst directly at his torso, sending him over the edge into the murky blood-stained water as well.

"I had him," Mike said as he wheeled around, his eyes blazing in fury.

"I know, but we need to get to the villa, we don't have time to waste on him," Jack said calmly.

Reining in his anger Mike remembered the boat they'd seen leaving the yacht earlier and recalled Petrov's words. He knew Jack was right; still choked by anger and adrenalin, all he could do was nod in agreement.

They both headed back for shore in silence, both men praying they would be in time to stop Petrov's men.

CHAPTER TWENTY-ONE

Rourke got off the train at the end of the line. He was walking through the streets on his way back to his temporary accommodation when his burner phone rang.

Knowing it could only be one person, he opened it and said, "Go ahead," without formality

"Tyler should be hard at work by now, so I want you ready to collect the item from him. I want you to go to the location I've sent you and wait," the voice said.

"Copy that," Rourke replied, ending the call.

———

Jack phoned Bainbridge on the way back to their temporary SI6 Headquarters in Stalida.

"Sir, we have a sit-rep. Mike and I made contact with the local Mafia leader, Grigori Petrov. It seems he left the Russian Mafia some time ago and has been in the employ of a group calling themselves H.A.T.E.; it's an acronym for the Hierarchy for Anarchy, Terrorism, and Extortion. It seems their reach is quite extensive."

"How extensive is it?" Bainbridge asked, concern evident in his voice.

"I got the impression it could be global, sir. I'm honestly not sure that it was a bluff. Petrov seemed quite confident."

"Where are you now?"

"On our way back to the villa. Petrov sent some goons to send a message to other clients about the price of rebellion. I'm afraid we could be too late to be of any help, they left some time ago."

"I'll inform Tony. What about Petrov? Is he still in play?"

"No, sir, we sent him and his very expensive yacht to Davy Jones' Locker. It was a terrible waste, but I like to send messages too."

"As soon as you've assessed the situation at the villa, I want the two of you on the Gulfstream heading back here. Is that clear?"

"As crystal, sir, and thank Major Bacon for his little going away present," Jack said, ending the call.

Glancing across at Mike, he noticed his friend seemed to be lost in his own private hell. The feeling of helplessness Jack felt at the thought of what might've happened at the villa had to be far worse for Mike. If the worst had happened, Jack hoped, for the men's sake, that they were long gone, if they weren't, the hell Mike would unleash on them wouldn't bear thinking about.

"Hang in there, Mike; we don't know what the situation will be until we get there."

Mike looked at his friend, his brows nearly touching, rage still filled his eyes. "Then you'd better get us there, and fast!"

———

When Bainbridge put the phone down, he sat thinking about what he'd just learned.

H.A.T.E., a new player in town, this was an interesting development, he mused. Picking the phone back up, he decided to give Tyler a ring to see if he knew anything about them.

———

Tyler heard the insistent ringing of his phone but ignored it. A quick glance at the screen showed who was calling.

"Damn it!" he said in frustration when he saw Bainbridge's number flash up. He knew there wasn't time to take the call; he was so close to getting what he needed, any little distraction put his daughter in even more danger.

He had to finish before he talked to Bainbridge. The man had a nasty knack of being able to tell if someone was lying or hiding something from him. In his heightened state of anxiety, he knew he wouldn't be able to disguise his fear for his daughter. No, he couldn't talk right now, he only had a few minutes left, he had to focus.

———

Bainbridge put his phone away, a frown creasing his forehead. It was not like Tyler to not answer his phone. Was there something going on he was not aware of? With that thought at the forefront of his mind, he called his Chief of Staff.

"Tony, where are you?" he asked when the call was answered.

"I was with the Armourer, sir, getting some practice

in on the firing range," Tony replied, sensing the urgency in his boss' voice.

"Come on up, there's been a development," Bainbridge instructed.

"On my way, sir."

Bainbridge put down his phone and sat thinking for a moment. If this Hierarchy was cleaning house, tying off loose ends, then who else was in the line of fire, he wondered?

CHAPTER TWENTY-TWO

Jack and Mike sighted the villa as they approached.

"Get ready," Jack prompted. Mike automatically reached for his Beretta and jacked the slide to inject a round into the breech.

Jack took out his Walther and did the same as he steered the car slowly up the road to the villa, not wanting to alert anyone to their presence.

"Look, they're still here," Jack stated, noticing a dark blue Peugeot parked near the front of the villa. It appeared to be the same vehicle they had watched the goons drive away in earlier that day.

Almost as if on cue, four men appeared by the door at the front of the villa. The utter lack of expressions on their faces made it evident that these were absolute professionals.

Jack suddenly pressed down hard on the accelerator gunning the engine and grabbing the men's attention. They roared up the driveway; a quick jerk of the steering wheel maneuvered the car parallel to the villa, allowing Mike to quickly drop out of the passenger's side the moment the car swung around using the vehicle as a shield to protect himself while he laid down cover to give Jack time to bail out and make his way around the car as well.

The men at the villa reacted swiftly to their sudden appearance; each drew concealed weapons from behind their back and opened fire, peppering the side of the car with bullets.

Jack instantly dropped to the ground firing his Walther between the wheels under the car as he aimed at the legs of the four men. His first shot dropped one of them, shattering an ankle. His second tore through the calf of another after it ricocheted off the ground, which slowed his escape.

Mike peered around the rear of the vehicle and fired his Beretta, hitting one man in the chest and sending him spinning to the ground, his weapon flying from his grasp. His second salvo tagged the last fleeing hitman in the shoulder and neck; he went down in a spray of arterial blood.

Jack and Mike rose from their place of cover, walking around the car to view their handiwork, guns extended, ready to fire should the need arise.

"What did you do to them?" Mike growled as he towered over the one with the shattered ankle. Jack stood close by, staring hard at the man that had been shot through the calf, his Walther aimed directly at his head.

The man peered up at Mike through pain-filled defiant eyes and said, "What we were told."

There was no remorse, just a simple statement of a job well done. Mike shot him in the head without a second thought.

Jack watched as Mike turned and went towards the villa.

"Stay there," he ordered the final assassin and, as he began to walk off after his friend, he fired his Walther ensuring the man would comply.

The two of them entered the villa cautiously; silently, they walked through the hallway, past the kitchen, and into the living area. The area was a wide-open space with stone tile floors, leather furniture, and a few framed photographs adorning the walls. In the center of the room, three kitchen chairs were positioned directly in front of a video camera that sat perched atop a tripod. Seated in the chairs were Georgios, Maria, and Nicos; each had been executed with one shot through the head. It had all been caught on camera.

This had been the message Petrov had wanted to send to the rest of his customers. This was the price you pay for rebellion.

Mike stood frozen, staring at the spectacle, whilst Jack slowly walked up to each of the bodies to check for a pulse to confirm what they both already suspected.

He walked back up to his friend, placed a hand on his shoulder, and said, "Mike, I'm so sorry, but this was not your fault."

Mike tore his eyes from the dead bodies and gave his friend a dubious look. "I was sent to help them, buddy, and they wound up dead. How is that not my fault?"

"You didn't pull the trigger, those guys outside did, you didn't cause this. If what I've heard of Georgios is true, he would've fought against Petrov anyway, and knowing now what we do about him, I'm pretty sure this would've been the result, with or without you. I know that's not much comfort right now, Mike, but it's a fact. This was not your fault; these two were on a collision course long before you entered the picture."

"You're right, buddy, that's no comfort at all," Mike said and walked off.

Jack took out his phone to call SI6 to give them another sit-rep. This time he was glad it didn't have to be him who gave Tony the bad news.

CHAPTER TWENTY-THREE

Tony stood looking at his boss's worried frown.

"What's up, sir?" he asked.

Bainbridge looked up, "I've just had a call from Jack in Crete. Apparently, Mike found out who was behind your friend's predicament, an ex-Russian Mafia bigwig by the name of Grigori Petrov. Have you heard of him?"

"Yes, sir, he's a very nasty piece of work. When you say 'ex', I assume you mean ex-Mafia, not ex-Russian?" Tony replied with a frown sensing something was coming.

"Yes, he's no longer associated with that group, he's found a new sponsor, something called H.A.T.E. It's an acronym for the Hierarchy for Anarchy, Terrorism, and Extortion. Ever heard of it?"

"No, sir, it's a new one on me."

"Get the R&D Division onto it right away. We need to discover everything we can about this group. If they're new players or not, we need intel on them if we're to fight them."

"Copy that, sir."

"I've tried to call Tyler to see if they have anything on them, but he doesn't seem to be answering his phone, which is a bit unusual, so we had better look into that too."

"Will do, sir. I'll send someone around to see him if you like?"

"Best take care of that yourself. I want to keep this as low profile as possible until we know more about this new group."

"I understand, sir."

"There's one more thing. Petrov killed your friends. He did it to send a message to others who decided to renege against his racket. I'm sorry for your loss Tony. I'm also sorry that, for the moment, you'll have to pay your respects to them from afar. We cannot be seen to be associated with what happened over there. It's an internal matter now, we'll send what intel we have to help the authorities, but we have to remain anonymous in this."

Tony looked down at his feet, gathering his thoughts. He had been friends with Georgios for years, now he was gone, and he couldn't even attend the funeral. Grief would have to come later though, what he needed to concentrate on now was getting whoever was responsible and making them pay.

He looked up from the floor at Bainbridge with hard, cruel eyes and said, "I understand, sir. It's the nature of what we do. If that's all, sir, I'll get onto R&D?"

"That's all, Chief," Bainbridge said, dismissing him.

Tony turned and left the room, his steps weighted down by the heaviness of his heart.

———

The Research and Development Division of SI6 was located in the lower levels of the Headquarters building. This was where all the testing and development of new technologies and equipment took place. It was also the central hub for computers and servers; access to every satellite in the world was linked through this location.

In charge of this Division was a rather remarkable individual.

"Ah, Colonel Armstrong, to what do I owe this pleasure?" Robert Deakin, a small man with thinning brown hair and horn-rim glasses, asked as he shoved his glasses up the bridge of his nose.

"I've been sent to ask if you know anything about a group called H.A.T.E. It's an acronym for the Hierarchy for Anarchy, Terrorism, and Extortion. Does it ring any bells for you?"

"I must say that this is a new one on me, Colonel," Deakin replied as he walked over to the computer on the far wall, "Let's see what our database has on them,"

The computer station had an array of monitors which allowed various events to be viewed via a live satellite feed.

Deakin's fingers danced over the keyboard as he input the search requirements. After a short while, he turned to Tony and said, "There's nothing I'm afraid."

"Are you sure? There must be something," Tony questioned, leaning forward to view the monitor for himself more closely.

"If there was something, I would've found it, you know that, Colonel. Are you sure you got the name right?"

"I'm positive. Take another look, go deeper, try the deep net and see what you can come up with about them.

Rumour has it they're not new players; they've been around for a while and are very dangerous."

Deakin saw the hurt in Tony's eyes and said, "I'll do what I can, Colonel, but it may take some time."

"Take as long as you need, Deakin, just be thorough about it, this is extremely important. Give me a call when you have something." Tony turned and left the room.

In this line of work, grief could be crippling. He had to lock the thoughts of his friends in Crete securely somewhere in the back of his mind. He would visit them again one day, but not yet, not today. Today he had work to do.

CHAPTER TWENTY-FOUR

Tony arrived at MI6's Headquarters on Vauxhall Cross and headed straight to Tyler's office.

The door was closed, so he knocked and waited to be invited in; no answer. This was strange, he was certain Tyler's secretary had said the Director was in and had been for most of the day.

"Deputy Director Tyler, this is Colonel Armstrong. I need to see you about something rather urgent; can you open the door, please?"

———

The sound of Tony outside his office meant he was out of time.

"Come on," he whispered nervously, "just a few more seconds."

He was almost finished downloading the NOC list to a secure flash drive then all he had to do was cover his tracks; no one could suspect him of being the one who had hacked into the server.

———

Leaning against the door to avoid being heard by others who might alert security, Tony said, "I'm giving you to the count of three, Director, if you don't open this door, I'm breaking it down."

As he began the countdown, the door opened.

"Colonel Armstrong, what can I do for you?" Tyler asked.

"I need to ask you about something. Can I come in?"

"I'm sorry, but now really isn't a good time," Tyler replied abruptly, blocking Tony from entering.

Tyler's phone rang, startling him. His eyes went wide as he checked the caller ID.

"I have to take this," he said, hurriedly pushing past Tony, holding his phone to his ear as he quickly walked off down the corridor.

Confused, Tony looked from the retreating figure of the Director to the door he had just opened, noticing something unusual, it had been left slightly ajar.

"That's odd," he thought, wondering what could possibly be so important to make the Director forget to close his door.

Making sure no one was watching, he quickly stepped inside, closing the door quietly behind him.

———

"I have it, what do you want me to do? I can't stay in my office, there's someone from SI6 snooping around," Tyler said into his phone as he walked.

"SI6, you say? No matter, they will be dealt with in good time. Get in your car and drive, I'll tell you where you're going once you're underway," Jones said.

"My daughter had better be there, or there'll be trouble."

"You are in no position to negotiate anything, Tyler. Let me remind you, you have in your possession a flash drive containing top-secret material; if you're caught with that information, you'll find yourself facing charges of treason, and the rest of your natural life would be spent in prison. You *will* do as ordered and nothing more. If you perform your task as instructed, I'll entertain the notion of freeing your daughter unharmed," the voice replied confidently.

A cold chill went down his spine as Tyler realized his mistake too late. He had given this Jones character total control; he *would* have to do whatever he wanted, whoever he was.

———

Once inside Tyler's office, Tony quickly noticed the Director's computer had been left on, the screen still active. Other than that, nothing seemed out of the ordinary.

"Let's see what he's been up to," he said to himself as he scrolled through a list of the Director's recent activity. Nothing seemed out of the ordinary there either. Deciding to call in some support, he took out his phone and called Deakin.

"I haven't got time to explain, Deakin, so listen carefully. I'm in Stuart Tyler's office looking at his computer. Can you remotely access it and see what he's been doing?"

"You want me to hack the Deputy Director of MI6's computer?" Deakin asked, his voice a full octave higher than normal.

"Yes, and I need it done now. Can you do it, or is this out of your league?" Tony goaded. He knew Deakin's ego wouldn't allow him to refuse the challenge.

"Of course, I can do it!"

The computer screen began moving like it had a life of its own. Screens opened and closed rapidly as Deakin remotely scoured through all the files.

"This is not good, Colonel," he said seriously.

"What has he done?"

———

Tyler drove with his Bluetooth headset firmly in place.

He had no idea where he was going. So far, his instructions appeared to be completely random, clearly, Jones wanted to keep him in the dark so he wouldn't have the chance to phone ahead and get a TAC team in place.

"There are abandoned warehouses near your location. Pull into the next one on your right, someone will be waiting for you," Jones instructed before the line went dead.

I'm here, he thought, suddenly realizing his location as he drove through an opening in a wall. Understanding dawning as the figure of a man came into view.

———

Tony rushed out of the Director's office, still talking to Deakin on his phone.

"Can you ping his phone? He was using it when he left here?"

"Sure, give me a minute and...yes, he's in the warehouse district in Deptford," Deakin replied triumphantly.

"Where are Mike and Jack when you need them?"

"Sorry, Colonel, I didn't quite catch that," Deakin said.

"Don't worry, Deakin, I was just mumbling to myself. Thanks, and good work," Tony replied, ending the call. Once again, he dialed Headquarters, but this time asking for Bainbridge.

"Sir, we have a problem," he said when the call was answered.

"Go on," was all Bainbridge said.

Tony quickly relayed everything, informing him what Tyler had done."

"I'll get a TAC team over to his location; I want you there ASAP to take command. This is a disaster, Colonel. If that list gets into the hands of the Hierarchy, then all our agents will be compromised."

"I'm on it, sir,"

CHAPTER TWENTY-FIVE

Tyler stopped the car and slowly got out. He had taken out a Sig P226 from the glove box and put it in his belt at the small of his back as an insurance policy before leaving headquarters. Seeing Rourke standing there, he knew he would need it.

"Sean Rourke, I've read your file, quite impressive," he said, closing the car door.

"Cut the chit chat, Tyler," Rourke replied coldly, "I understand you have something for me."

"Tell me one thing first, why did you turn?" Tyler asked, desperate to stall. There was no sign of Mary.

"What makes you think I turned?" Rourke replied with a hint of a smile.

"You're a sleeper?" Tyler questioned, not quite believing this turn of events himself. He fired off, "who... the Russians, Koreans, Al Qaeda?" He had to know, his professional curiosity taking over.

"No one you've ever heard of Tyler. We've been hiding in the shadows for years, or so I'm told. I honestly have no idea how far back this really goes; I just know that it's old. Now, give me the flash drive."

"Who are you working for?" Tyler asked with deadly calm as he pulled the Sig free, intending to aim at Rourke. Before he even had a chance to raise his gun, a searing pain rocketed through his right shoulder. The force of the bullet from Rourke's gun as it ripped through spun him around; his numbed fingers were no longer able to retain their grip on the gun as it clattered uselessly to the ground. As fast as he had been, Rourke had been faster. Tyler fell to the floor in a heap, helplessly watching Rourke as he approached.

"You want to know who we are, I'll tell you. We are H.A.T.E., the Hierarchy for Anarchy, Terrorism, and Extortion. I'm only telling you this because, like your daughter, you'll never leave here alive."

Realization of his daughters' fate fired rage in Tyler's eyes that was quickly snuffed out by the bullet from Rourke's gun as he aimed and fired one last time.

Tyler slumped to the ground, his head a bloody mess of shattered bone and tissue, slowly pooling beneath him. Rourke knelt by his side, carefully searching the contents of his pockets for the flash drive.

As he rose, he retrieved his phone dialing Jones.

"It's done; I have the flash drive, and Tyler's with his daughter."

"Excellent work. Make sure the flash drive is safe. As soon as you can, get to a secure terminal and upload the contents to me. Then just sit tight and await further orders."

———

When Tony arrived on the scene, the TAC team was already in place. There was no sign of Tyler, his car, or anyone else.

"Over here, sir," shouted one of the team, kneeling to get a better look at something.

Tony didn't have to be told what the substance was; he recognized blood when he saw it.

"Blood," the TAC team member said as he stood.

Tony peered around the abandoned building, trying to see into secret corners. "I want every inch of this place torn apart. There must be something here, some clue. Find it."

As he wandered away from the scene, he took his phone to call Bainbridge, the General wasn't going to be pleased.

"There's no sign of Tyler, sir. He's long gone."

"Over here, sir," shouted another team member.

Tony turned to look; the man who had shouted was standing by a cellar with the hatch lid up.

"You're going to want to see this, sir."

Tony looked down into the hole. There was Tyler's body, it had been unceremoniously dumped on top of a young woman's corpse.

"I wonder who she is?" the man asked.

"His daughter," Tony said, turning away from the gruesome sight. Putting his phone to his ear once more, he informed, "We found him, sir. Tyler's dead. They must've used his daughter as a threat to blackmail him— get the list, or they'd kill her. Her body's here too. He must not have known she was already dead. Obviously, they don't take prisoners, and now they have the list."

"There's nothing we can do now except wait to see if they want something. Have the team remain on site until a clean-up team arrives. I'll inform the PM. You may as well return to HQ, Tony."

"Copy that, sir."

———

Rourke sat on the edge of the bed in his hotel room next to the laptop Jones had provided. Jones had ensured it had been loaded with a military-grade security suite and extra strong firewalls for further protection.

He inserted the flash drive into the USB port and waited for the upload to complete. Once the upload was completed, he saved a backup copy of all the files as a precaution before sending everything as an attachment to an email address given to him specifically for this purpose. He waited for confirmation that the message had successfully been sent before closing the laptop.

All he had to do now was wait for his next set of instructions.

CHAPTER TWENTY-SIX

Tony walked into the General's office with a sour look on his face.

"Take a seat, Tony. I can tell by your expression you feel the same as I do about this whole mess," Bainbridge said as he rose to his feet and walked over to a cabinet in a corner of the room. Retrieving two crystal tumblers into which he generously proceeded to pour a deep amber coloured whisky.

"Is it that obvious, sir?" Tony replied, plopping himself heavily into one of the wingback chairs in front of the General's large mahogany desk.

"I'm afraid so, son. Here take a sip of this, might help improve your demeanor somewhat," Bainbridge urged as he offered up the glass.

The General seated himself once more, took a sip of the amber twenty-year-old single malt, and after a short pause, looked at Tony. "I feel the same as you; I hate it when we come up short in these things. Good people have died needlessly, and many more are in danger. We were unable to prevent this from happening."

The desk intercom buzzed, interrupting Tony's reply. Bainbridge reached across his desk to press the button on the intercom opening the channel. Immediately, Jen said, "Sir, you need to look at your computer, now."

Bainbridge activated the screen in front of him; a message was emblazoned across it. It read

I have in my possession the NOC list taken from Deputy Director Stuart Tyler of MI6. If you don't allocate one million pounds sterling for each name on that list to be delivered to a bank account of my choosing, I will be forced to release the names. You have twelve hours to comply. If you have not completed the transaction by then, I will release four of the names, and the price will go up to two million per name. Every hour you fail to comply after that, another four names will be released, and the price will double per name again and so on, until either you pay my demands or there are no names left to release. To show that I will do as I say, I will release four names in one hour. You can save the other hundred souls by collecting my fee and getting it ready. I will be in touch before the first deadline to see if you have seen sense and to give you details of where to send the money.

Mr. Jones.

The message moved in a continuous loop as it repeatedly scrolled across the screen, ensuring the message was read and understood.

Bainbridge sat back in his chair, completely unaware he had been leaning forward as he read the screen.

"What do you think, sir? Do you think this is a serious threat?" Tony asked.

"I have no doubt this is serious. What puzzles me though, is who is doing this."

"Do you think it's this Hierarchy?"

"It's beginning to look like that, which brings up another question."

"What's that, sir?"

"Why now? If they've been active for God knows how long and they've kept hidden, why are they making themselves known now? Why come out of the shadows and let us know they exist? Surely they'd have been better off, unknown?"

"I see your point, sir. It does pose a quandary."

"How soon before Jack and Mike arrive?" Bainbridge asked.

"Another three hours, I'd say, sir."

Bainbridge opened the intercom, "Miss Austin, who else was linked to that transmission?"

"It appears it was transmitted on every computer screen, sir," she replied.

Bainbridge looked at Tony, "Get Deakin on this right away, see if he can trace the IP address of whoever streamed this. We need to find them and shut them down! Tell him he has one hour before the first four names go viral. I want Jones' address well before that."

Tony was out of his seat like a shot and heading for the door before Bainbridge had finished speaking.

———

Deakin was well into his search for the perpetrator by the time Tony reached R&D.

"Talk to me, Deakin. What have you got and make it plain English?"

Deakin was hunched over his keyboard, his fingers abusing the keys as he typed furiously, all the while continuously checking the array of monitors before him.

"Nothing yet, Colonel, but I'm narrowing it down.

This guy thinks he's really clever, he's re-routed the signal through various other servers around the world in the hope it will be untraceable, but he made one fatal error."

"And what was that?"

"Coming up against me, of course," Deakin said arrogantly, as if it were obvious.

"Well, now that you've made that statement, you'd damn well better find the little creep hadn't you."

Deakin paused as if the thought of failure had never occurred to him, he glanced quickly at Tony and then immediately began working again with an even greater fervor. His reputation was at stake now, for him, that was far more important than the lives that could be lost.

Tony watched as screen after screen flew across the various monitors, he couldn't make heads or tails of the information flying by. Deakin, however, was in his element; a smile slowly stretching across his features, evidence that he was truly enjoying the chase. This was what he lived for; the one-time infamous hacker now found greater satisfaction chasing down other hackers just to prove, in fact, he was better than any of them.

Tony's phone rang. Moving to the back of the room so as not to disturb Deakin, he answered the call, "Go ahead, sir," he said when he read the caller ID.

"I've just had the Director of MI6 on the phone. Apparently, they had the same message, which seems only fitting seeing as how it was their NOC list. He was apoplectic, had absolutely no idea that Tyler had been turned. He said he was only just hearing of our involvement in the Goff scenario himself, seems Tyler kept that one close to his chest. He's informed me that they'll try and send out recall messages to all their agents, but some are in deep cover and won't be able to get out easily.

There's simply no way they can get them all out in time, Bainbridge said.

"It's a mess, alright, sir. Deakin is hot on the heels of whoever is behind this, but it'll take time."

"Time is something these operatives do not have, I'm afraid. Tell him to double his efforts, we must have that location before the first hour is up," Bainbridge said, disconnecting the call.

Tony looked at the time on his phone, only fifteen minutes left. There was not much time left before the first four names would be released.

CHAPTER TWENTY-SEVEN

"There's been a development here. Tyler was coerced into giving up the NOC list to a third party, who we suspect could be this Hierarchy. Someone has been in touch and demanded one million for every name on the list, or they'll start to release the names in batches of four. To prove they are serious, they're going to release the first four names in less than fifteen minutes. We're currently trying to find the location of the IP address to prevent them releasing any names, but so far, it's not going so well," Tony's voice came through loud and clear on speakerphone.

Jack looked at his friend, noting the concern on his face. If those names were released, not only would the operative's lives be at risk, those they loved would be at risk as well, not to mention the damage done to all the operations they had taken part in. Months, maybe even years, of hard work and sacrifice would be gone with one keystroke.

Jack listened as Mike asked, "Is there anything we can do, sir?" They were powerless to help until they landed at the airport. What then, though? He was supposed to be leaving SI6, this was supposed to be his last job.

How could he turn his back on them now though? If Melissa couldn't understand this then maybe she wasn't the woman he thought she was.

His decision made, he said, "There's nothing we can do until we land, sir."

"You're right, Jack. Report back to HQ as soon as you land. I'm hoping we'll have some better news for you by then."

From his peripheral, Jack saw Mike looking at him smugly; he wore an expression he knew all too well.

"Don't give me that look. You know very well I'm always pulling your arse out of the fire, one more time won't hurt."

"If you say so, buddy, just don't tell Melissa this was my idea, right. I don't want her coming after me," Mike chided, looking away as he spoke to hide his smile.

"Don't worry; she'll be too busy kicking my arse around to worry about you. There's nothing we can do anyway for the next hour or so. Let's just hope they have it all under control by the time we land."

———

Tony was still in R&D when Deakin turned to him, looking deflated, "I'm not going to have the address in time."

Tony checked the time; they only had three minutes left on the clock.

"Keep working, there's still time yet," Tony said.

Deakin knew better than to argue, taking a deep breath, he returned to his task with an urgency he hadn't known he possessed but froze in his tracks when the main screen before them unexpectedly stopped all activity. One by one, four faces appeared on the screen, the names belonging to each one scrolled past, stopping under each face. Now each face had a name attached.

"Shit!" Deakin said when he saw them.

Tony slammed his hand down on the desk, "Damnit, we've run out of time."

———

Sean Rourke had just finished cleaning his weapon when his phone rang.

Eagerly he snatched it up.

"It's about time. I was going stir-crazy sitting here waiting," he snapped.

"I understand you've been working for a colleague of mine," an unfamiliar voice said.

"Who is this?" Rourke asked.

"Who I am, is of no concern to you, Mister Rourke. What I want to know is..." the voice replied in a steady calm manner.

Rourke realized, by the way this man spoke, he was someone used to getting their own way and quickly collected himself, "Go on, I'm listening."

"...I understand you've been working for someone known to you as Mister Jones. What you should probably know is he has made some questionable choices of late for which he will be held directly accountable. He has single-handedly brought attention to our organization after years of working behind the scenes. He is solely responsible for exposing our existence to the security services of the United Kingdom and, no doubt, soon, the rest of the world. What I need to know now is where your loyalties lie. Is it with Jones or the Hierarchy?"

Rourke replied, without hesitation, "The Hierarchy, sir."

There was a pause, the line went so quiet Rourke thought he'd lost the connection. After a moment, the stranger said, "Good, carry on as normal, continue with any and all instructions Jones issues but be ready to act when I give the order. Is that clear?"

"As crystal, sir," the line abruptly went dead.

Puzzled, Rourke put his phone away as he thought about what he'd just learned. It seemed this Jones character, whoever he was, was a bit of a maverick and was about to be called on the carpet for it. What he personally knew about the Hierarchy he could put on a postage stamp. Clearly, the top of their agenda had always been their anonymity; Jones' recent actions had ruined all that and judging by this call, they were *not* happy, to say the least.

It wouldn't be hard to lie to Jones about what was going on; as a double agent, he'd learned to lie proficiently years ago. It was going to be interesting to sit back and watch events unfold from here on out.

He sat down and held his phone ready; it was just a matter of time before Jones called with instructions for the next stage.

——————

Tony was frustrated with Deakin's lack of progress tracking the hacker's IP address.

Irritated, he shot off, "You said you almost had him, what's the holdup?"

"He's really good, but I almost have him. I've deleted most of the bogus servers he's routed his signal through, but this takes time. There are literally thousands of them, and I have to make sure I get every single one."

"Look, Deakin, four of our operatives have just had their names blasted all over the internet. Now, the terrorist groups they've infiltrated will know their real objective and kill them on sight. I don't want to have to sit by idly and watch while another four names are released. Get it done, fast," Tony said urgently.

Deakin turned, looking ready to argue.

"What the fuck are you looking at me for? Put your eyes back where they belong and find that sonofabitch!"

CHAPTER TWENTY-EIGHT

Mister Jones was feeling rather pleased with himself.

Everything seemed to be going smoothly after the initial hiccup over the NOC list. He had everything in place, the Security Services of the UK had no choice now but to capitulate to his demands. He was confident they would not allow any further agents' names to be revealed; he was just as certain that he had covered his tracks thoroughly; they would never trace anything back to him. Leaking the name of the organization was a risk. He was fully aware his superiors valued their anonymity, but he was gambling that the security services would want to keep it a secret too. They would not want any other countries or criminal elements to know they had been bested by an unknown organization; they needed their reputation to remain intact.

He had been working for the Hierarchy for the past ten years, working his way through the ranks toward the top ever since. He had been recruited at a seminar where he found his views correlated with some of the ideals the Hierarchy found important. Jones, of course, was not his real name; in the real world, he was Samuel Greenberg, an aide to one of the members on the National Security Council.

His phone rang, startling him out of his reverie; it was the entity known only as Number One, the head of the Hierarchy.

"Sir, to what do I owe the honor?" he asked.

"Jones, you have overstepped your purview with this mission," the voice on the other end said flatly.

"I don't understand, sir, to what are you referring?" Greenberg queried carefully.

"Do *not* insult my intelligence, Jones. I know everything you have done and are about to do. Did you think the Hierarchy wouldn't keep an eye on our operatives to ensure anonymity?"

"Sir, you don't understand. I can explain," Greenberg pleaded.

"Were you not the one in charge; were you not the one in control? I understand everything perfectly. You exposed our presence to those we fought against for years. Maintaining our anonymity is how we became so strong, so powerful; no one knew we even existed. Now, the Security Services of the UK can't stop talking about us, looking for us, digging into who we are, and *that* is all down to you. *That* is a crime that must not go unpunished."

Greenberg felt his world beginning to collapse all around him. The organization had people everywhere, their power was immense, and now that power was going after him. There was nowhere he could go.

Instead of catapulting himself to the forefront of the Hierarchy, his gamble had backfired. He had signed his own death warrant.

"I have their NOC list. They will pay me, they will

pay us, one hundred million pounds sterling to get it back. My death would achieve nothing," he desperately argued.

"It will serve as a reminder to others, the Hierarchy does not applaud failure, we punish it."

"What about my operation? I need to see it through, this *will* work. The finish line is too close now to hand it over to someone else, I have to do this!"

"Yes, you do," Number One said, pausing, "this operation has become a damage limitation exercise. Do you think that if you pull this off, you will have earned yourself a stay of execution?"

"Perhaps, at least, give me the chance to redeem myself?"

"Okay, for the time being, you will be allowed to remain on point for this operation and have the full backing of the Hierarchy, but if you fail, if the UK Security Services catch up with you, then you *will* be disavowed. I'm certain you understand the meaning of that word, having worked with the Security Council, you understand all the ramifications,"

"I thought you would be pleased, this organization stood for anarchy, terrorism, and extortion. With this operation, I have given up the names of four agents, causing anarchy. This act of terrorism achieved what it was meant to, plus we are extorting a huge amount of money when they buy the list back. You tell me, does that not live up to the tenets this organization was founded upon?"

"It does, and admirably, but you miss the point entirely. The shadows have been our security; we have survived and thrived there in the dark; our best strategies have stemmed from there because no one can see us. You have single-handedly thrust us under a spotlight. Now, every police force, every security service around the globe can target us and fire at will. We are now the prey instead of the predator. We need to get back into the shadows where we can survive and fight another day."

"I agree, and I apologize," Greenburg conceded.

"I will be in touch," and then there was silence.

Greenberg immediately knew what he must do, he quickly gathered what he needed and set about putting his plan into motion. He dialed Rourke's number, "Here are your new instructions. You are to escort a vital member of this operation to his home in Scotland. His name is Samuel Greenberg; he has been working closely with me in this operation. You are to ensure his safety at all times, is that understood?"

"Clearly, but what is his role in this?" Rourke asked.

"He is the broker in the upcoming deal with the authorities; you must keep him safe. Be at the location I am texting you now in fifteen minutes, a car will be there to pick you up. Bring everything you need with you, leave nothing behind."

"Copy that, fifteen minutes," Rourke replied.

CHAPTER TWENTY-NINE

Rourke was reading the text with the location when his phone rang

"Yes?" he said, putting the phone to his ear.

"Jones has been ordered to complete this operation. MI6 and the other services know of us; that can't be helped right now, but we can limit their knowledge of us. I want you to keep watch over Jones. Keep him safe until this is over, you are his personal minder until then," the voice said.

"He's just contacted me with instructions to look after a Samuel Greenberg, who will act as broker in the deal with the authorities. I'm to be picked up in fifteen minutes; we're going to his home in Scotland."

"Stay with him, follow his instructions, and above all, keep the list safe. Our Mister Jones *is* this Mister Greenberg."

"Copy that, sir," he said.

Alex Berg was not a man who could blend into a crowd. At six-feet-six, he was a mountain of a man with broad, muscular shoulders and the body of a pro wrestler.

He was an ex-Army Rangers squad leader who was cashiered out due to disciplinary reasons. He had problems with authority figures, an unfortunate result of a cruel upbringing by an abusive father. The incident that got him expelled from the only institute that he ever respected involved an argument with a fellow officer. The end result of the argument was several broken bones, a wired jaw, a shattered kneecap, and the end of a military career for the officer recovering in hospital.

Berg quickly found another profession where he could vent his pent-up rage—as an enforcer for the mob. His talent as an enforcer garnered him attention from a certain organization that preferred complete anonymity.

The phone he held in his hand rang once.

"Yes!" he said, answering it immediately, his ice-cold blue eyes constantly scanning his surroundings as he spoke.

"You have a new assignment," the voice on the other end said.

"I'm listening."

———

"I have him," Deakin said, excitedly pumping a fist in the air in triumph.

Tony was by his side in a flash, his phone to his ear, ready to make the call.

"Where?" he asked simply; every fiber of his being was eager to get moving, to do something, anything.

Deakin looked up at him, "He's here, in London," he said, his eyes wide in disbelief.

Tony looked at him, "Where exactly?"

————

Alex Berg arrived in Edinburgh by train. Exiting the station, he walked to the nearest taxi.

"Take me to the Smithfield Hotel," he instructed once he had squeezed his immense frame into the rear seat of the vehicle.

His orders had been specific, take a room in a quiet hotel and await further instructions. He sat back in the seat and looked out of the window as the driver pulled out into traffic.

Edinburgh had long been one of his favorite cities, and he relished the opportunity to return, even if it was for only a few days.

————

"The IP address belongs to Samuel Greenberg, he's a junior aide to one of the members of the National Security Council, sir," Deakin said hesitantly.

"Are you sure?" Tony asked.

"I've checked and double-checked; then I checked once more just to be certain. It's him, Colonel."

"I'd better inform the General. This has just gotten very tricky," Tony observed.

"That's an understatement," Deakin muttered as Tony spoke into his phone.

"General, we have that address. You're not going to like it."

CHAPTER THIRTY

A few minutes later, Tony was seated in the rear of a staff car next to Bainbridge on their way to Greenberg's residence.

"What are you planning to do, sir?" Tony asked.

"Confront him, of course. We have evidence tracking the release of the four names from the NOC list to his computer, therefore, it's reasonable to assume he has the list," Bainbridge replied.

"What about his connection with the government, sir? Won't that be a problem?"

"Not when his employer learns what he's done. He'll be thrown to the wolves; no member of parliament would want to be associated with anything like this."

"I hope you're right, sir."

Bainbridge noticed Tony's worried frown, "What's bothering you, Tony?"

"I'm not sure, sir. This just seems too easy. It just seems odd that anyone who could plan and put this type of operation together would work from home. That's just too easy. It doesn't feel right somehow," Tony explained.

"He probably never expected anyone to find him, got overconfident. It's the weakness of an educated mind; they often think they're cleverer than everyone else. It's going to be his downfall."

"I hope you're right, sir."

"We'll soon know, we're here," Bainbridge replied, pointing to the three-story Victorian townhouse they had just pulled up in front of.

The two men walked up to the front door. Bainbridge rang the bell, nothing happened. He rang again.

The door to the house adjacent creaked open, and a little old lady popped her silver head around the frame, curious to see who it was.

"If you're after Mister Greenberg, I'm afraid you've just missed him. He packed a few bags and drove off a few minutes ago. I suppose he's heading off to his place in Scotland, you know, the one he's always talking about," she said breathlessly, her voice old and scratchy.

The two men glanced at each other, "And what time would this have been, approximately, Miss?" Bainbridge asked.

The old lady smiled coyly at the 'Miss' remark, "Around a half hour ago, I suppose, although it could've been longer. I never took that much notice, you know."

Tony tried to disguise a smirk as Bainbridge politely said, "Thank you for your time, you've been most helpful."

As they climbed back into the car under the careful scrutiny of the inquisitive neighbor, Tony said, "Didn't take that much notice? I bet she even knew what color his bags were and what was in them."

"Get in contact with Jack and Mike's pilot on the Gulfstream. Tell him to redirect to Scotland. Maybe we can get a break here with this titbit; they just might be able to get the drop on him. He won't be expecting anyone so soon, if at all," Bainbridge said before instructing the driver to take them to Fairfax airfield.

"I take it we're going too, sir," Tony observed.

"Yes, I want to confront this bastard myself. We may need some extra bodies on deck though. Something tells me that if Greenberg is, in fact, this Jones fellow, he may have some serious backup."

"What're you thinking, sir?"

Bainbridge had an evil glint in his eye as he said, "I know Commander Dark of the SBS happens to be in Scotland at the moment with 'C' Squadron. If they're not too busy, I think I'll second their help in this just to be on the safe side. I'm interested to see how the Hierarchy handles Commander Dark and his friends in the SBS."

"Good idea, sir," Tony agreed.

CHAPTER THIRTY-ONE

Commander Johnathan Dark was indeed in Scotland with members of 'C' Squadron, overseeing a close protection duty operation for a prominent politician who wanted his visit to Scotland to remain anonymous.

Dark was six feet three with broad shoulders and a lean, rock-hard torso. His dark hair and flashing hazel eyes, which seemed to shine from a rugged face, gave the impression of an immovable stone wall. He was the epitome of solidity. The Commander was someone who could be relied upon in a crisis, no matter the conditions. He had led 'C' Squadron for the past four years; at the moment, he wasn't happy.

The close protection duty assignment was not going as he would have liked.

Their assignment was to guard a member of the government who was meeting with a member of Sein Fein in order to pass over delicate information. If news of this meeting was ever leaked, then the lives on both sides would be put in danger.

Scotland had been chosen simply because it was

accessible for both parties quickly, and it was also out of the way enough to allow the meeting to take place without anyone else's knowledge, or that was the plan, at least.

The venue was a small hotel on the Isle of Arran situated on the south coast. The Kildonan Hotel was perfectly situated, being far from any crowded cities while providing stunning coastal views. The white-fronted building overlooked the bay, with its restaurants featuring the best views. The meeting itself took place over a quick lunch in the restaurant whilst John and the three members of 'C' squadron patrolled the grounds, casually scanning the grounds for any potential threat, blending in completely to remain unobserved by any of the other guests. Once lunch was concluded, the meeting moved outside where the two men could take a leisurely stroll in the garden, eventually pausing beneath the gazebo, a spot where they could talk freely, while John and his companions made sure they remained undisturbed.

"What's up John, you've got that look again?" asked Dave Hawkins, the smallest member of the group. His hawk-like eyes never missed a thing; he'd noticed his commander's attitude change the moment the two men left the restaurant.

"This doesn't feel right somehow, it's too easy," John replied softly. They were communicating through a radio network; the discrete earbud he wore acted as both receiver and mic.

"I've learned to trust your instincts, Boss, they've gotten us out of a lot of sticky places, but too easy isn't what I expected," Hawkins said.

Just then, three men exited the restaurant and began walking purposefully toward them.

John heard their approach and turned to look at them, his instincts flaring to life. "Here we go," he said.

The three approaching men wore long coats completely unsuited to the warm weather. As they got closer, each man threw open his coat to reveal automatic rifles.

"Guns!" John shouted as he drew his pistol, instinctively aiming and firing the Sig Saur 230 in one smooth motion. The .380 caliber shells unerringly found their target's heart, dropping the first man dead in his tracks.

The second and third men had already opened fire on the two delegates of the meeting, but Hawkins and Smith had already reacted to the threat pushing the two men down to the ground to relative safety.

Bullets flew, peppering the gazebo and sending tiny chunks of wood and splinters into the air.

Panicked screams from the other guests reached them from the garden, but they had little time to worry about that, their priority was clear.

John dove to the side just as one of the shooters aimed in his direction, narrowly avoiding the line of fire. Rolling out of the dive, he rose up on one knee, already aiming his Sig at the shooter, rapidly firing three times. The first bullet hit the man's stomach, the second connected high on his chest, and the third shell decimated the assassin's right eye as he buckled under from the previous impact.

Smith and Hawkins stood their ground, covering the two delegates who remained on the ground, their guns aimed at the last shooter who had been taken out by Sanders, the fourth member of the protection detail.

"What just happened here?" Walter Simmons asked as he struggled to his feet. His eyes wide as he watched the men assigned to protect him check the bodies to ensure all threats had been eliminated.

"We just saved your life, sir," John replied calmly as he approached.

"Who were they?" Donal Murphy asked, his voice a little shaky.

"I was hoping you could tell me," John replied, spearing him with an intense stare.

"What, you think I set this up, man?"

"Did you?"

"I risked my life to bring you this list. I'm a dead man if they ever found out," Murphy sputtered.

"You didn't deny it though."

"Are you out of your tiny little mind? Why would I risk bringing you a list of active members of the group and then send someone to kill me?"

"Because you knew they wouldn't, and it would give your story plausibility."

"I knew this was a mistake, you Brits are all the same. I shoulda' listened to my Ma," Murphy replied, looking away from them.

"You told your mother about this meet?" John asked incredulously, his eyebrows going up into his hairline.

Murphy looked at him, then his expression altered, his brows knitted together, and his teeth clenched, "Are you accusing my Ma of sending these guys? I'm her son, for Christ's sake?"

"Who else knew?" John asked, his voice rising in frustration.

"No one, I told no one. I'm not an idiot," Murphy retorted acidly.

"And yet you told your mother, who still has ties to the old order," John countered sarcastically.

"She remembers what it was like back then, all the

killing. She'd never do this," Murphy denied, shaking his head.

"Could she have told anyone about you going away today?" John probed more quietly, trying a different approach.

"What are you saying?"

"Well, I agree that she may not have sent those guys, but someone did. Is it possible she may have mentioned it simply in passing to someone who passed that information on to whoever did send them?"

Murphy reluctantly thought about that for a second, frowning. "I did overhear her talking to someone about me not being able to help with something. I think Sally was moving house, the council finally found her a place and she wanted to know if I could help with the move. Ma told her I was away today."

"Who's this Sally?"

"Sally Maguire," he said, his eyes widening in understanding.

"There you go. If she told her father you couldn't help, he'd want to know why. He'd definitely do some digging, and I bet he found out where you were going. There's your leak," John reasoned.

"I'm a fucking dead man," Murphy said despondently, slumping down on one of the wooden seats.

Walter Simmons said, "I'll organize protection for you. I'll make the call and get a team over here right away. We'll have you back on the mainland in a few hours."

He turned to John, "Good work, Commander, my boys will take it from here."

John nodded his head in agreement as he waved his team off to allow Simmons' already approaching security detail to take control of the scene.

The phone in his pocket rang.

Quickly he retrieved it, answering it before the first ring ended with, "Yes?"

It was Bainbridge, "Commander Dark, I do hope I've not caught you at a bad time."

"If you're calling me, General, then it's a bad time for someone, no doubt. What can I do for you?"

Bainbridge succinctly filled the Commander in with all the salient points necessary to make an informed decision.

"Are you available?" Bainbridge asked after a short pause.

"As it happens, General, me and the boys have just finished up here. We can be wherever you want as soon as you forward me the details."

"Excellent, I'll text you the address where I want you to go. I'm on my way as we speak and will meet you there; we should be there in a few hours."

"You're coming too? This must be important."

"You have no idea, Commander, no idea," Bainbridge said, ending the call.

As he put his phone away, John muttered, "How did he know I was in Scotland? This was supposed to be a secret." Louder, he shouted to his men, "No rest for the wicked guys, we've got another job."

CHAPTER THIRTY-TWO

Mike and Jack were sitting quietly in the comfort of the Gulfstream when the chirp of Mike's cell phone sliced through the relaxing atmosphere.

Noticing who the caller was, he answered immediately, placing the call on speaker, "What is it, Colonel?"

"You've been diverted to Scotland. We know now that Samuel Greenberg has the list. He's a member of our government, working as an aide to a member of the National Security Council. He's currently on the run, heading to his estate in Scotland; I'll text you the address. We're en route ourselves. When you arrive, you'll be met by Commander Dark of the SBS. He and members of 'C' Squadron will act as backup. If this Greenberg has ties to the Hierarchy, we can expect he'll have some serious backup himself, so be prepared."

Jack asked, "When you say you're en route, who do you mean?"

"Myself and the General, he wants to confront Greenberg personally."

"Copy that, sir, just make sure he keeps his head down when the shooting starts."

"I'll be fine, that's why I brought you boys along," Bainbridge interrupted through the connection.

"With all due respect, sir, we can't be expected to do our jobs properly if we're looking out for you as well," Jack added.

"Point taken, once the shooting starts, I'll make sure I'm out of the firing line. Will that do?" Bainbridge countered.

"I suppose it'll have to, sir," Jack agreed.

"Okay then, we'll see you all there," Tony said.

Jack looked into the eyes of his friend across the table from him, "Back into the fray as they say."

———

Berg was getting fed up of sitting around waiting. He'd been in Edinburgh for some time now, and nothing seemed to be happening.

He was a man of action dammit; he needed to be doing something, anything. Sitting around waiting only made his mood darker.

He had just decided to go for a walk to burn off some energy when his phone rang.

"Yes?" he said, concealing his eagerness.

"Here are your orders. Go to the ancestral home of Samuel Greenberg. He is in possession of the NOC list recently obtained from MI6. A double agent named Sean Rourke will be acting as personal security for Greenberg; you are to take control of the security of the estate. The British Security Services are looking for this list, and I'm sure their investigation inevitably will lead them to Greenberg. Until he has completed the operation of extorting the fee from the British Government, he is to remain safe. If the operation turns sour, then terminate both Greenberg and Rourke. Leave no loose ends for the authorities to investigate. Is that understood?"

"Fully, sir, is that all?"

"Yes. Greenberg employs staff loyal to us with whom you will be able to form a viable defense against any intrusion, use them wisely."

There was an abrupt 'click' before the line went dead.

Finally, he had something to do, something he could sink his teeth into. He quickly gathered his things and began making plans.

CHAPTER THIRTY-THREE

Rourke had been picked up, as ordered, by a driver of a black Bentley limousine. He was shown into the rear seat, where he met Greenberg, who was already sitting comfortably there.

As he slid into the comfortable seat, he looked at the man opposite him, a small man with a shock of thinning light brown hair. He was in his late fifties with a weathered face, like a map made from parchment that had been scrunched up. His eyes were nothing more than mere slits, he could barely make out their color, but he guessed they were slate grey. His crumpled suit attested to his hurried and harassed demeanor. By his side lay a laptop case, over which he draped one hand protectively.

"I've been led to believe your name is Sean Rourke and you're here to ensure my safety, is that correct?" Greenberg said by way of greeting.

"That is correct. Mister Jones gave me specific instructions; I'm to follow your lead and ensure your safety while you're acting as a broker in this deal over the NOC list. Is that still correct? Has anything changed?"

Rourke replied as he made himself comfortable in the leather seats.

He watched as the man before him gave him the once over; it was almost like he was coming to a decision over something. When he finally spoke, he averted his eyes, a dead giveaway.

"Actually, it has. I received a call from our Mister Jones as we were on our way to pick you up. The deal has changed; he has instructed us to hold an open auction for the list. Anyone interested may bid; he's provided me with a list of names he would contact with the details."

"But I thought you were extorting the British Security Services for the list," Rourke said.

"That part of the plan has not changed, this just gives them more of an incentive to come up with the money," Greenberg replied with a wry smile.

Rourke leaned forward in his seat, "Or it could just give them the incentive to come after us with everything they have. Has Jones thought of that?"

"I can assure you, Mister Jones has thought of everything," Greenberg said, his smile slipping slightly.

"You don't seem so confident," Rourke observed, noticing the subtle change in Greenberg's demeanor. Something was off, and he couldn't quite put his finger on it, like an itch with the sweet spot just out of reach.

Greenberg's face straightened as he looked out of the window; clearly, Rourke's words had rattled him.

The car continued at a steady pace, the driver obviously not wanting to draw attention to them. After about half an hour, they pulled into an abandoned warehouse district. In a clearing where several buildings had been flattened, a helicopter waited; its rotors turning slowly.

"Our ride is here," Greenberg announced, his smile returning. Rourke quickly peered out the window, his eyes wide for a second. "You didn't think we were going to drive all the way to Scotland, did you, with the Security Services alerted to our plan?" Greenberg said, reaching for the door handle.

Once outside, Rourke watched as the smaller man walked over to the waiting chopper, hunching to avoid the rotor wash, quickly motioning for Rourke to follow.

As he strapped himself in, he noticed Greenberg signal to the pilot to get underway. The power from the engines surged through the fuselage of the craft as the rotors spun more violently. Soon they were airborne, heading north to their final destination.

Leaning in closer, regardless of the headsets both men wore Greenberg shouted, "I want to arrive as soon as possible, we have much to prepare. I understand your concerns, but I have faith in the power of the Hierarchy."

"I hope you're right," Rourke said as he turned to watch London slipping away beneath them.

———

Jack and Mike landed at a remote private airfield in the Highlands. The only building present was a small shack which had a huge array of antennas on its roof; obviously Air Traffic Control radar set up to provide clearance for any incoming or outgoing flights.

As the two men deplaned, they noticed another plane parked on the tarmac nearby as well as two men standing restlessly by the shack.

"Looks like they got here before us," observed Jack.

Mike surveyed the barren landscape. There was nothing but mountains as far as he could see and not another soul in sight other than those he had already seen.

"It's gonna be a long fucking walk getting from here." he muttered. As if in response to his complaint, two Land Rover Discoveries entered the compound, driving directly to the shack.

Bainbridge exited the lead vehicle as it rolled to a stop, immediately walking in their direction, closely followed by several other men with military bearings.

"Allow me to introduce your backup, Commander Dark, and members of 'C' Squadron of the SBS," Bainbridge said as they quickly approached.

"I think we'd better get a move on, gentlemen, if we want to get on station. It gets dark early up in this region," John said, shaking all the offered hands.

"You heard the man, let's get moving," Bainbridge ordered, ushering them all towards the two waiting vehicles.

"I think our odds have just gotten better," Mike said with a wry smile.

Jack gave his friend a deadpan look, "I'm not sure if things have got better or just got worse."

CHAPTER THIRTY-FOUR

Rourke looked out the window as the chopper carrying them cleared a range of mountains; there was a vast expanse of nothing as far as the eye could see.

"When do we reach your estate?" he asked.

"We've been flying over it for the past half hour," Greenberg replied, indicating a small building in the distance. "That's my home, there."

Rourke looked where Greenberg indicated. At first glance, he saw nothing but a speck, but as they got closer, the speck grew into a huge building. A true mansion with several floors and God knew how many bedrooms, Rourke estimated upwards of fifteen. It had spires sitting on top of end sections giving it the appearance of a European fairy-tale castle. Parked at the rear of the property was another helicopter, this one was a military gunship.

Rourke glanced at him and said, "If I knew you had this much money, I'd have asked for a raise."

"If we survive this, consider that your year-end

bonus," Greenberg replied, motioning toward the gunship.

As the chopper descended, Rourke looked out the window once more, thinking about the task set before them.

As the chopper set down before the mansion, he quickly unbuckled his seatbelt and opened the door for them to exit. As he admired the grounds of the lavish gardens, he noticed a hulking man stalk towards them from the front of the building.

"Greetings, gentlemen. I've been instructed to handle the estate's security. My name is Alex Berg, Number One sent me."

"Glad you could make it, Berg. What plans have you made for me?" Greenberg said with a sideways glance. It was obvious he didn't trust the newcomer.

"I've set up a perimeter guard, and the yacht in the harbor nearby is ready for your departure. I thought you could continue your business transactions from there. It would be safer than the residence, and it has the means to transport you further away should the need arise. I have lookouts stationed on all the roads and anywhere an entrance could be considered. If anyone comes near, I'll know," Berg told him confidently.

The big man looked at them both with the eyes of a predator; Greenberg was wise not to trust him.

"That sounds pretty extensive, you seem to know your job," Greenberg said.

"I do," Berg agreed, reaching for his phone as it rang.

"We have two Discoveries en route to the residence, looks to be at least four in each vehicle," a voice said.

Rourke deduced, from Berg's sudden stern expression, the call was not good news.

"Trouble?" he asked, "Anything we should be made aware of?"

"We have visitors," Berg said, putting the phone back to his ear. "Hold them off as long as you can, I'm coming in the chopper."

"How the fuck did anyone get here so fast?" Rourke muttered, glancing at Greenberg, who seemed cool and calm.

Greenberg sighed, "It was always a matter of time before they found out who was behind this,"

"Well, time has just run out. Rourke, you take Greenberg down to the harbor, get him on the yacht. It has the latest in communication gear, so whatever he needs to do, he should be able to do it there. In the meantime, I'll take care of this," Berg said.

As Rourke ushered the smaller, older man towards the harbor, he watched the behemoth as he marshaled more men towards the gunship.

"Come with me, sir," he said as he turned his attention to what he was doing. "Let's get you aboard that yacht."

CHAPTER THIRTY-FIVE

"What's that?" Jack asked, craning his neck to look out the window.

Mike listened, "Sounds like a chopper."

"Are we in contact with the other Discovery?" Jack asked the soldier sitting in the front passenger seat.

"Yes sir, we are," he replied.

"Tell them to watch out, I think we're—" Jack's sentence was cut off in mid-flow as the attack chopper swooped in low from the side, strafing them with 50cal shells from the twin cannons on board; the first pass narrowly missed the two vehicles.

"Get us outta here," Mike shouted.

Jack strained to catch a glimpse of the chopper.

"There, it's hovering," he said, pointing out of the window as the aircraft pivoted around to face them. Twin puffs of smoke billowed from the pods as the rockets were launched toward the vehicle.

"Incoming!"

Like a shot, the driver spun the wheel as far as

possible as he simultaneously stamped on the accelerator. The vehicle surged forward, swinging violently to the side, careering out of the way of the rockets.

Jack twisted around as best he could from his precarious position in the upturned vehicle to see where the rockets were heading. He saw the twin smoke trails seconds before they made impact with the ground right where they would have been had the driver not acted quickly.

The shockwave from the blast threw the passengers back against their seats as torrents of dirt were catapulted into the air, clods of dirt and rock were smashed into the vehicles as debris rained down around them.

———

John glanced around, noticing the other vehicle was in the same shape.

"We have to get out of here, fast," he shouted, quickly unfastening his belt in order to scramble for the door. He contorted his body so he could apply enough pressure with his shoulder against the door to force it open. He braced his legs against the seat and pushed, heaving the door open against the added weight given to it from the angle they were sitting in the dirt.

He squeezed out of the small opening, finally allowing the door to slam shut. As he drew his pistol, he looked up and spotted the chopper coming back around for another run at them. He glanced down at his pistol thinking, *"This isn't going to be enough."*

———

"Take us back around, I want to finish them off," Berg curtly ordered the pilot through the headphones.

He was in full control of the weapons, allowing the pilot to concentrate fully on flying the chopper.

The two Land Rover Discoveries were lying, upended in the dirt directly below them; figures were just beginning to emerge from beneath the wreckage.

"There they are. The cannons should suffice this time," he said, providing a running commentary to his actions.

He readied himself, his finger on the trigger as the chopper turned and began its run.

———

Jack pulled himself free from the upturned vehicle and quickly ran around to the rear, retrieving the kit bag; he ripped it open, grabbed an HK MP5 from inside it, and tossed it to Mike.

Catching the rifle in mid-air, Mike pulled back the lever injecting a round into the chamber.

Jack readied his own weapon and glanced at his friend, sharing a brief smile before they both focussed on the approaching chopper.

In his periphery, Jack saw Smith and Sanders, the two other SBS men, climb free from the front of their vehicle; they, too, were retrieving weapons from inside.

"Time to rock and roll," Mike shouted above the din of the rotors.

All four men aimed their sub-machine guns at the chopper, letting loose a withering hailstorm of bullets. Sparks flew as the bullets lit up the exterior of the chopper, causing the pilot to steer the aircraft out of harm's way.

"That's what I'm talkin' about! You run off to your momma, you muthafucka," Mike snarled through gritted teeth as he watched the chopper turn tail and run.

"Good work, men. Now let's get these vehicles righted before that chopper decides to return," Bainbridge said, startling Jack, who hadn't heard him approach.

They had just finished getting both the Discoveries back on their wheels and were leaning against the vehicles, getting their breath back, when Jack spotted the chopper coming back around.

"Here it comes," he said, swinging his MP5 up to fire. He'd already inserted a fresh mag into the sub-machine gun in anticipation of the chopper's return.

Jack stared at the chopper; it didn't seem to be moving.

Motioning toward the vehicles, he said to Bainbridge, "Get in and get moving, that thing's going to fire rockets any second. We'll hold it off, you head down to Greenberg's place and stop him."

The General nodded and turned to his men, "Tony, Commander, grab one of your men, you're with me."

Jack and Mike, along with the remaining two SBS men, Sanders and Smith, took cover behind the remaining Discovery.

Jack opened fire first on the hovering chopper; the rest followed suit, laying down cover as the others sped away in the other ATV; their tires kicked up a trail of dirt as they spun and left.

Jack stared down the sights of his sub-machine gun, wondering if he'd get to see his wife and daughter again as the butt of the MP5 kicked against his shoulder.

———

Berg looked down at the small group cowering in the meager cover the wreckage of the Discovery afforded them and smiled.

"I've got you now," he said, firing the rockets.

CHAPTER THIRTY-SIX

Commander Dark sat in the front passenger seat of the escaping ATV, his hazel eyes dark with fury.

He didn't like leaving men behind, and it showed.

As their vehicle crested a ridge, they could see the mansion below. John half-turned as he heard an explosion somewhere behind them.

He felt a warm hand on his shoulder, "Don't worry about your men, they're in good hands. My boys are the best there are, and if anyone can get out of there alive, it's those two," Bainbridge assured him.

"Copy that, sir," he replied, unable to bring himself to say anything else for fear of revealing his true feelings. Instead, he concentrated on the job at hand and focused on what was ahead of them.

"What do you think we'll find down there, Tony?" he heard the General ask.

"I'm sure the Commander has a better idea than I do, sir. He's been in more of these situations than I have, I would imagine," replied Tony.

"I know this much, sir, whatever trouble we may face,

I'm bringing along a whole lot of pain," John said through gritted teeth.

———

The four men were huddled against the far side of the Discovery when the rockets hit. The twin blasts threw the ATV into the air as though it were nothing more than a child's toy, sending it spinning over their heads.

Knowing the ground would divert some of the force from the blast, Jack threw himself into the dirt, instinctively covering his head with both hands. He fell in an attempt to force his body as close to the ground as possible, hoping the tremendous winds caused by the blast would streamline over him rather than pass through his body, pummelling him.

He felt the impact of the ATV landing as it crumpled on the ground a few yards away, breathing heavily with relief realizing, if he could breathe, that meant he was still alive.

The smile he wore as he stood quickly faded as he saw the chopper fly pursuing the fleeing second Discovery.

"Come on, we have to get down there," he shouted as the others climbed to their feet, unscathed as well.

———

Berg watched as the rockets hit pay dirt, admiring the resulting twin blasts that lifted the already battered ATV into the air. He had seen four men cowering behind the stricken vehicle; they were an easy target, one he simply could not pass up.

Confident he had taken the target out, he waved to the pilot to go on.

"Time to finish this," he said, switching his attention to the other Discovery approaching the driveway to the mansion.

————

The Discovery slid to a halt in front of the huge red brick mansion. The occupants poured out, running for cover just as the chopper flew overhead, 50cals blasting divots out of the walls.

"Fuck me, that was close, sir," Hawkins said to John as they leaned against the doorjamb inside the massive hallway.

"Yes, it was rather," Bainbridge agreed, "I'm beginning to think I may be a little too old for this type of operation."

"It is a young man's game, sir," Tony agreed.

"For now, let's just get this job done, shall we?" John said, his eyes widening.

"They won't leave us alone for long, sir," Tony said as he caught his breath, "I expect them to land that chopper and try again."

John looked around. They were currently in the hallway; in the middle of the hall stood a huge wooden staircase that stretched up to the first floor, where it branched out before carrying on to the floor above. He craned his neck just enough to see around the column currently sheltering. To the left were two doors, mirrored by a twin set of doors on the opposite side of the room.

All these potential hideaways for someone to spring an attack on them made his skin go cold.

"Sir, we need to move and fast," he said, looking straight at Bainbridge.

The General nodded in agreement as he labored to get his breath back.

"Do you know where the target will be?" John asked hopefully.

"Haven't a clue," Bainbridge said flatly, dashing any hopes he had of a quick completion to the job.

"We'll just have to do it the old-fashioned way then," John said. Suddenly the woodwork overhead was peppered by bullets.

———

Rourke was pushing Greenberg along the jetty to the yacht moored in the harbor when he heard another set of explosions go off.

"Things are certainly heating up," he said, glancing back at the house over his shoulder.

"Get me to the yacht quickly," Greenberg said hurriedly, "I can upload the list to a satellite and then transmit it to wherever I want."

"And you honestly think that'll stop them?" Rourke said skeptically.

"No, of course not, but we won't be here. Once we're on board, we set sail and head for the open seas. Once we're in International waters, they won't be able to touch me. The auction will go ahead as planned, and the British Security Services will be powerless to prevent any of it from happening," Greenberg informed, his lips turning up in a devilish smile as he stood with his hands on his hips.

"I have to admit, that could work," Rourke agreed, nodding his head. Looking back at the mansion, he added, "We just need your men to hold them off a little longer."

CHAPTER THIRTY-SEVEN

John ducked low as the hail of bullets threw chips of wood and plaster into the air around his head.

"Holy shit!" he exclaimed as he rolled forward, firing his gun in the direction he thought the bullets had originated.

An agonizing scream told him his aim had been true. Kneeling low, he gestured for the others to begin moving towards the staircase; as he followed, another hail of bullets struck the floor where he'd been just a few seconds earlier.

"Okay, we need to move further inside and find where Greenberg and Rourke are," John said, taking the lead. It was a role that came naturally to him.

"How many hostiles do you think we're facing?" Tony asked.

John glanced around the staircase they used as cover. His eyes took in every nook and cranny, judging where the best defense would be and along with the most likely spots for snipers to hide, if there were any.

"I'd say no more than three in this section; I can't

judge the rest of the house though. If we clear this section, we should be able to move forward with relative ease."

"Unless those from the chopper get here first," Tony reminded him.

John looked at the Colonel and winked, "We'd better get a move on then."

"Right, on my signal, we move towards the back. That's probably where they headed to get away from the gunplay," John said, preparing to move.

He swiftly moved away from the staircase, rapidly firing a burst in the direction of the original gunfire.

John waited a heartbeat as the shooter ran behind the staircase towards the rooms at the back of the house, waiting for his moment. The shooter stopped for a moment, then popped out to fire, giving John a good look at his target. A swift double-tap ended the stand-off as the bullets took the top of the shooter's head off, knocking him back against the wall in a mist of blood and gore.

Without hesitation, he sprinted after the others, quickly catching up with them.

"Where to now, Boss?" Hawkins asked as he surveyed the area with his MP5.

"Any suggestions General?" John asked.

"We need to find Greenberg, or better yet, the NOC list," Bainbridge said.

"I doubt the list will be very far from Greenberg," John said, looking around for any sign of anyone.

"It doesn't look like there's been much traffic through here recently. Doesn't Greenberg have a yacht, sir?" Tony asked as he followed John's eyes around, looking for the same signs.

"A yacht, you say," John replied, knowing right then precisely where they would find them.

"Out the back, this place has access to the coastline, that's where he's gone. He has his yacht tied up at the back of his property, he'll be going there, and I wouldn't be surprised if he's heading for open waters where we won't be able to touch him," John said.

Before any of them could move, another hailstorm of bullets peppered the woodwork near John's head.

———

Jack, Mike, Sanders, and Smith ran toward the mansion.

"The chopper's landing," Jack said through gritted teeth as he ran.

"We're too far away, out of range for these MP5s, we need to get nearer," Mike said angrily.

Nothing else needed saying; each man doubled their efforts to reach their friends in the mansion below.

———

As the chopper landed, Berg removed his radio headset, hanging it up as he opened the door and jumped to the ground, making sure to keep his head low to avoid the rotor wash.

His earpiece mic squawked moments before he heard a voice.

"We have them pinned down, sir," the voice said over the sound of gunfire.

"Good, keep them occupied, I'll be there shortly."

———

"Holy shit, that was close," John said, having barely moved his head in time to avoid the salvo, knowing they were pinned down.

Hawkins said, "What now, sir?"

John looked around, checking their options. They were slim. What made it worse was he knew that chopper would return soon, bringing their opposition reinforcements.

He glanced at something on the wall close to where the gunman stood, and an idea began to form. It was a long shot, but anything was better than remaining where they were, waiting to get gunned down.

"I have an idea," he said, walking out from behind their cover, his MP5 raised to his shoulder, ready to fire before anyone could say a word.

He fired a single shot at the fire extinguisher he'd spotted mounted to the wall. The bullet pierced the container sending a cloud of fire retardant throughout the area, obscuring the gunman's sight.

"Right, let's move," John said urgently, prompting the group to sprint towards the back of the house using the gas cloud spewing out from the extinguisher as cover.

As they cleared the rear of the mansion, running out into the estate's expanse of garden, they couldn't help but look around.

"Wow, this is some spread he has here. Just how rich is this bastard?" Hawkins asked, whistling through his teeth.

The lawns were immaculate; towards the rear of the garden was a gate that led onto a path from which the harbor could be reached. In the distance, John spotted the yacht, a Fairline Targa 53GT, a modest-sized luxury yacht easily capable of maneuvering in and out of the

Lochs in Scotland. It appeared not only nimble but speedy too.

John could just make out two figures on the top deck going towards the bridge.

"They're on board already, we're too late."

In absolute frustration, he emptied his clip at the boat, helplessly watching as it pulled away from its moorings.

By the time he'd reached the landing, the boat was already in the bay, heading for open water.

Staring at the boat, hands on knees as he gulped air painfully into his lungs, he said, "We lost them," to the others when they caught up to him.

Tony stood next to him, fighting to catch his breath as he searched for something, anything. It was then that he saw what just might enable them to pull this one out of the fire.

"Not yet, we haven't," he said.

John looked up at him, then followed where his eyes were looking, and a knowing smile slowly crossed his face.

CHAPTER THIRTY-EIGHT

Jack, Mike, and the two SBS soldiers were almost at the mansion when Jack's phone rang.

"Little busy here, trying to get to your location," he said on the run, his voice a little shaky from his exertions.

"We have a situation here, and here's what I need you to do," Bainbridge responded.

Jack listened intently as Bainbridge explained their plan in detail.

"Copy that, sir; we'll be in position in about three minutes."

Jack continued silently running once the call had ended until Mike spoke up, "What the hell was that all about, buddy?"

Jack filled everyone in on what the new plan was, they were nearly at their destination by the time he'd finished.

"Do you think that'll work?" Sanders asked.

Jack looked at the three of them, "We're about to find out."

"Take cover!" John shouted as gunfire rained down on them from the mansion.

Tony grabbed Bainbridge and pulled him away from the line of fire.

John and Hawkins dove to the ground as they returned fire, hoping the other two would have sufficient time to get to cover.

Tony dragged the General towards a small boat shed near the end of the jetty. Once he knew the General was safe, he peered around the edge of the shed, adding his own fire to the others, trying to give them the cover they needed to join them.

John and Hawkins kept low as they ran for the shed.

"Jeez, Boss, that was a close call," Hawkins said, a little breathless as he pressed his back to the shed.

"What are our options now? It seems to me that we are pinned down with nowhere to go," Bainbridge observed ruefully.

"Don't count your chickens just yet, General," John told him.

Bainbridge looked at the Commander as the gunfire started up once more, sending wood chips flying into the air.

"Well, whatever you have up your sleeve, now would be the time to pull it out."

———

The chopper sat alone near the front of the mansion, its rotors turning slowly as the engine idled.

"Right, let's do this," Jack said.

He and Mike went one way whilst the other two soldiers went in the opposite direction.

Jack made sure he was clearly visible to the pilot, who remained in his seat.

"Hi, there!" he said, giving him a friendly wave.

The startled pilot reached for a sidearm.

Jack held both hands up, showing he was unarmed, as the pilot brought his pistol up to fire, but before he could squeeze the trigger, Mike was at the cockpit door yanking it open.

The pilot froze, his eyes wide with shock at the sight of a gun barrel aimed right at his head.

"Boo!" Mike said, pulling the trigger. The pilot's head exploded across the front of the chopper's windscreen.

"I'm not cleaning that up," Sanders said as Mike pulled the body from the chopper.

Jack climbed into the co-pilot's seat, asking, "You do know how to fly this thing, right?"

Mike wiped blood off the controls and cleared off some of the windscreen as he settled himself in the vacated pilot's seat. "Do bears shit in the woods?" he replied.

"Right then, get this thing in the air."

Mike adjusted the controls and soon had the chopper airborne, flying over the rear of the mansion before they knew it.

"You two lay down some covering fire for our guys," Jack said to Smith and Sanders in the rear passenger compartment.

The soldier's 9mm rounds slammed into the rear of the building, causing those inside to take further cover.

———

Alex Berg saw the chopper fly over. A keenly honed instinct earned over years on the firing line alerted him to danger.

Something was not right here; he'd given the pilot strict orders to stay put.

Suddenly bullets began raining down on them from the passenger side. Had he not listened to his instincts, he would have fallen foul of the salvo the same as three of his men.

Quickly he marshaled the rest of his team, instructing them to retreat. He returned fire with his MP5 and was satisfied when the two gunmen moved briefly back inside.

The chopper moved away, giving him a short respite before a new barrage of gunfire erupted from a different direction.

It was the group he thought he'd already pinned down.

This was rapidly turning sour on them.

———

John spotted the chopper as it came over the top of the mansion.

"Get ready," he ordered.

The instant he saw Sanders and Smith open fire, he signaled for Hawkins to follow his lead.

The fire they laid down forced those in the mansion to retreat, his signal to move.

With Hawkins close at his shoulder, they moved out from the cover of the boatshed, MP5s at their shoulder, ready to fire.

John saw the big man step forward, open fire on the chopper, and his bullets pepper the side of the aircraft.

"Oh no, you fucking don't!" he muttered through gritted teeth opening fire on the man.

———

"Right, get me over that yacht," Jack said, watching as the hostiles retreated into the mansion.

Mike maneuvered the chopper, turning it towards the water where the yacht was moving off.

Everyone felt the aircraft shudder under the impact of gunfire coming at them from the ground.

"Sonofabitch!" shouted Sanders, who was nearest to the doorway.

"You two okay back there?" Jack asked over his shoulder.

"It'll take more than that to scare us off," Smith said, earning a fist bump from Sanders in agreement.

Jack faced the front once more, a smile playing across his face briefly. "Okay, get me as close as you can to that boat. It's time we paid them a visit," he said.

"Copy that, buddy."

———

John and Hawkins ran crouching towards the rear of the mansion, firing their MP5s in short bursts to reserve ammo.

The others were being picked off one by one as they retreated further inside.

He saw the big man look around as his forces were being depleted by the superior marksmanship of their attackers and decided it was time to change tactics.

John knew he was almost there, just a few more steps

to reach them, when he saw the big man glance to his side and then down at a fallen merc.

John felt his blood run cold when he saw the big man suddenly stand, reaching for a small object that he threw in their direction. Reacting instinctively, he dove for the ground shouting, "Grenade!"

CHAPTER THIRTY-NINE

Rourke stood on the flying bridge listening to the sounds of battle coming from the shore; Greenberg was busy setting up the uplink connection to the satellite for the upcoming auction down in the main lounge.

Rourke watched as the chopper joined the battle; when it suddenly turned in their direction, he quickly turned and ran down the stairs to the main lounge inside.

Greenberg looked up from what he was doing. "What?" he asked.

Rourke spat out, "We've got company."

———

The grenade exploded, throwing huge clumps of dirt into the air as John lay on the floor by Hawkins; both men lay with their arms covering their heads to protect themselves from the deafening explosion.

Briefly, John thought about Bainbridge and Armstrong; he hoped they had heard his warning in time to take cover, but he didn't have too much time to worry about that at the moment.

Shrapnel peppered his body painfully after the shockwave passed; he didn't have time to worry about how severe his lacerations were right now; he would worry about that later when this was all over, if he survived.

Once everything had cleared, he glanced up from his prone position, a huge man was bearing down on them fast.

"Oh crap!" he muttered, working to bring his MP5 up to fire.

A huge hand suddenly wrenched the weapon from his grasp, tossing it across the ground away from him. He felt himself being dragged to his feet until he was staring into the ice-cold eyes of a killer.

John watched as a meaty fist drew back, ready to fly straight at his face; adrenalin coursed through him, instantly replacing the dizziness he felt from the concussion of the blast as he prepared to fight the monster off.

His only course of action, in the position he was in, was to head butt the man. Rearing back, he smashed his forehead against the bridge of the monster's nose, watching with satisfaction as blood began to gush forward from the force of the blow; the giant staggered back, releasing his grip.

There wasn't a second to waste.

Immediately John swung a swift right-left combo.

Berg covered up defensively, roaring his anger as he charged forward, tackling John, slamming him to the ground.

John's vision filled with stars as the wind was forced from his lungs in an explosive gasp.

If he didn't do something quickly, this behemoth was going to kill him.

———

"Get the crew to repel boarders," Greenberg shouted, adding with a smile, "I've always wanted to say that."

Rourke immediately obeyed, shouting over his shoulder as he left, "You may regret saying that when the shooting starts."

Quickly the crew of three armed themselves. Back on deck, Rourke took up a position close to Greenberg, pistol ready.

Things were about to get interesting.

———

"Hold her steady over the rear deck; I'll drop in on them there" Jack instructed as Mike steered the chopper closer to the yacht

"Copy that."

Noticing activity on the deck of the vessel below them as its crew suddenly began appearing, Mike shouted to the men behind him, "You guys back there are gonna need to give Jack some cover, or he'll be dead before he hits the deck."

The two SBS soldiers quickly positioned themselves by the chopper door as Jack grabbed hold of the rappel line, preparing to drop down as soon as they were in position.

A barrage of bullets from the vessel below peppered the side of the chopper, forcing him to retreat back inside the chopper for cover.

———

Rourke watched as the chopper made a low approach hovering over the rear deck. From the deck, he could see three figures sitting closely together by the opening. Two of the men were holding MP5s, obviously preparing to lay down cover for the third, who intended to rappel to the deck below.

"Open fire!" he shouted; the crew obeyed, letting loose with everything they had.

———

John lay flat on his back, immobile, as he stared up at Berg. The hugely muscled man smiled briefly, knowing he had the advantage as he used his weight to keep the man below him pinned, preventing him from escaping. Unexpectedly, Hawkins's figure came into view, flying from the side as if out of nowhere, tackling the behemoth and giving John the moment's respite he needed to get to his feet.

Hawkins rolled on the ground, trying to gain an advantage over the big man, but it was no contest. With a grunt, the big man thrust his arms up, tossing the SBS soldier from him like a rag doll.

The strength and speed of the monster was incredible. Without thinking, John rushed him; the giant of a man just smiled up at him.

It was clear by the man's face that John wouldn't be getting another chance at him, he needed to level the playing field, he quickly sprang to his feet.

"God, the bastard's fast," John thought as he dodged another punch intended to take his head off.

Ducking quickly inside the big man's reach, John buried two punches deep into the wall of the giant's rock-hard abs. *"God!"* he thought, *"I may as well have hit a brick wall."*

Berg countered with a swooping right hook that sailed over John's head, passing so close he felt the displaced air move his hair.

Rapidly he fired another barrage of blows to the man's midriff, this time closer to the kidney area, hoping to inflict some damage.

Berg grimaced in pain as the second punch landed on the small of his back.

"Paydirt!" John thought, following up with an elbow to the same spot causing Berg to arch his back and giving him the opportunity to charge the giant, sending him staggering forward.

Out of the corner of his eye, Hawkins shakily got to his feet; next to his feet on the floor was his fallen MP5. Quickly, John crossed to him to retrieve the weapon when he saw the man's eyes go wide in horror.

Instinctively he knew it was too late.

CHAPTER FORTY

Jack's face was splattered with blood inside the relative safety of the chopper as Sanders took several bullets to the chest, landing on his back by Jack's side; one look in the man's eyes told him all he needed to know.

The gunfire below continued as Mike sharply banked the chopper away from the barrage of bullets, heading towards another target.

A scream cut through the air of the fuselage, followed by a sudden lurch as the chopper lost control.

Mike had been hit.

Jack exchanged glances with Smith, both men silently acknowledging what had happened, bracing themselves as the chopper spun out of control. The centrifugal force of the rotation pinned them against the bulkhead, powerless to do anything except wait for the impact.

"Come on, you fuckin' bastard!" Mike shouted above the roar of the engines, somehow battling through the pain of his gunshot wound to regain control of the chopper.

The shooting from the yacht below had ceased as

Mike struggled to regain control. Obviously, the chopper's tailspin had convinced those on board the yacht that they had done enough to finish them all off.

Jack vowed to prove them wrong as he sent up a silent prayer; for a moment, the chopper righted itself. It seemed Mike had successfully regained control of the beast. Jack relaxed for a second, breathing a sigh of relief just as the engine cut out and the chopper plummeted to Earth.

———

Tony stood watching the exchange between Commander Dark, Hawkins, and the big man with rising apprehension. The behemoth was looking to be unstoppable, easily handling the two SBS soldiers.

He wanted to join in the fight, but his main purpose at that moment was to ensure the safety of General Donald Bainbridge, his commanding officer when he saw the giant draw a gun and aim it at John's back, he knew he had to act.

Bringing up his own pistol Tony aimed and fired, satisfied when the bullet slammed into Berg's back just below the left scapula spinning the large man around and redirecting his aim, allowing John just enough time to get to his feet and put the big man down.

———

Rourke knew Greenberg had kept the yacht stationary just offshore so he could acquire a stable uplink to the satellite he was using.

Spying the chopper as it came hurtling towards them out of control, Rourke turned, running into the lounge shouting, "Take cover!" to Greenberg, who was furiously working away on a special laptop.

Greenberg looked up from the keyboard and opened his mouth to speak just as the vessel was rocked by the impact of the chopper.

The entire rear section of the yacht was submerged by the impact, causing the nose of the vessel, where Rourke and Greenberg had been taking cover in the lounge, to shoot into the air. The velocity of the sudden lift acted like a catapult as Rourke was thrown into the ceiling of the lounge with a bone-jarring impact, temporarily disorienting him.

Freezing water quickly invaded the lounge through large holes ripped into the hull.

Rourke watched as Greenberg gathered himself, his eyes unfocused, from a probable concussion.

"Did you do it?" he shouted.

Greenberg simply shook his head.

Was Greenberg simply clearing his head or saying he wasn't responsible? Rourke wasn't precisely sure, but it was absolutely clear this mission was over. His main priority now was survival; it was leave now or drown.

A trickle of blood on the side of the older man's head caught his attention as the cold water hit his system, shocking him. He watched Greenberg stagger, the man was uncoordinated and delirious. Finally, he collapsed, sinking under the rapidly rising water.

Quickly grabbing the laptop, Rourke headed towards one of the openings, his arms and legs moving in relaxed strokes as he swam free of the sinking yacht, fighting against the current that threatened to pull him under.

Jack braced himself the best he could when he saw the water coming up fast.

"This is going to hurt," he thought as they crashed.

The impact hurled the passengers around like rag dolls.

Jack watched helplessly as Sanders' body was sent flying through the open door into the water. He and Smith desperately held on to the rigging inside the chopper to prevent the same from happening to them.

Blood trickled down Jack's forehead from an injury he suffered when his head struck the bulkhead on impact.

The front of the chopper was in the worst shape, it had taken the brunt of the impact. *Is Mike still alive?* he wondered.

"Take care of the crew, I'm going to check on Mike," he informed Smith, immediately checking his volume when he realized by the expression on the other man's face that he was shouting, *"My hearing must've been impaired from the impact,"* he thought silently.

Mike's body was easily visible as he pulled himself forward into the cockpit, his head lolled to one side where he sat still strapped to his seat; blood trickled down his cheek from several lacerations, most likely caused by glass from the shattered windscreen.

"Mike, wake up, man. We have to get out of here," he said urgently, shaking his friend by the shoulder in an attempt to rouse him.

"What the fuck!" Mike muttered groggily, looking around with unfocussed eyes at his predicament, quickly grimacing from the pain that shot through his right shoulder from the bullet wound that bled freely.

Jack removed his shirt to staunch the bleeding.

"C'mon mate, we need to get you out of here," he said, cutting Mike free from the harness.

"Smith get one of those dinghies into the water," he ordered, "Mike's coming to you."

"What about the crew on the yacht?" Smith shouted back.

"Your priority now is to make sure Mike gets to shore," he responded. "I'll take care of those on the yacht."

"Copy that," Smith said, immediately ripping an inflatable free from its moorings.

Several minutes passed before Jack and Mike finally stepped free of the chopper to board the raft.

Once inside the inflatable, Jack passed over a first aid kit to Smith.

"Apply an emergency dressing to his wound; we'll get it looked at more closely when this is all over," he told Smith.

Taking a quick moment to look around, Jack noticed the rest of the yacht's crew abandoning their posts and swimming for shore.

"Take the raft out to a safe distance and wait for me, I'll be right back," he shouted to Smith before setting off deeper into the rapidly sinking yacht. There was little time left, he had to get to Greenberg and stop him from releasing any more names off that NOC list.

———

Berg stood, unfazed by the shots fired at him, stopping John, completely stunned in his tracks.

"Fuck me!" he said under his breath when the big man simply smiled at him.

"Don't worry, I intend to," was all the giant said before running at John like a freight train.

Quickly John drew his pistol, instinctively aiming at

the middle of the man's body, he fired. Hoping for the best, he was relieved when he saw the bullet strike Berg just below his collarbone, stopping him in his tracks. Without waiting, he rapidly fired three more rounds, watching as the big man staggered backward from the impact of each bullet, breathing a sigh of relief when the giant's lifeless body finally toppled to the floor.

Adrenalin flooded through John's system. This was one of the few times he remembered ever being truly afraid. He'd never come across anyone like this monster before.

"C'mon, let's get to the shore and see what's going on down there," he said, motioning to Hawkins, who stood staring in awe at the downed behemoth.

"What the fuck was that guy made of?" Hawkins wondered aloud as he approached his commander.

"Concrete, I think, based on how hard it felt when I hit him," John replied with a smile as the two men quickly ran to join Tony and Bainbridge at the water's edge.

CHAPTER FORTY-ONE

Jack quickly ran through the yacht, using the walls to steady himself against the lurching deck. When he reached the half-submerged main lounge, there was no one in sight until a body he quickly recognized came floating towards him, it was Greenberg. There was no sign of Rourke or the computer.

He surmised Greenberg must have been using a laptop; Rourke must've taken it with him when he left.

The yacht lurched dangerously, taking on more and more water, sinking fast; he had to get out now, or he'd be dragged down with the yacht.

He waded toward the door feeling the pull of the deck beneath him as it sunk deeper; frigid water was flowing rapidly around his legs by the time he reached the deck beyond the door. He had less than a minute to get clear of the floundering vessel before he would be trapped in the spinning vortex caused by the sinking craft. Not time enough, he realized, but he had to try.

Jack launched himself over the railing into the open water away from the yacht, swimming for all he was worth in an attempt to get clear of the deadly undertow. He was only a few feet away, arms and legs pumping through the water, when the yacht gave one last sigh and finally sank beneath the surface. Doubling his efforts, Jack swam as hard as he could against the strong current to no avail. He could already feel himself being pulled back into the whirlpool created by the sinking yacht.

Still, he fought; thoughts of getting home to his wife and daughter flashed through his mind. He focused on keeping a promise he made the last time he saw them, fearing it was a promise he would break as he felt the water drag him down.

He fought against the pull of the current, focussing on the surface just above him, afraid he would never reach it. Hope was beginning to fade when a strong hand grabbed him by the shoulder, hauling him to the surface.

Gasping for breath, he looked up into the face of Smith.

"Hold on, sir, I've got you."

Jack had been so intent on escaping the sinking vessel he hadn't even noticed the small dinghy approaching.

Smith grabbed Jack's hand, hauling the exhausted man over the edge of the inflatable.

Jack lay there breathless, watching the churning water where the yacht had once been, unable to speak but with a huge smile on his face. He was going to be able to keep his promise after all.

When he was finally able to speak, he said, "We failed, Rourke escaped, and he has the list."

Smith asked, "How?"

"Over there," Mike motioned carefully with his head towards a figure struggling against the water to reach the shore, his efforts hampered by the laptop he was desperately trying to keep dry.

"Rourke," Jack said tightly.

"Right, sir, grab this; let's get after him," Smith said, tossing Jack an oar.

Rourke was lying exhausted on the shore as the men approached.

Leaping from the boat, Jack shouted toward Smith, "Stay with Mike."

Rourke struggled to get to his feet as he heard their approach, collapsing with the effort, too weak from his previous struggle to get to shore.

"It's over, Rourke. Hand over the laptop," Jack instructed as he aimed his Walther at him.

With great effort, Rourke slowly stood, keeping the laptop firmly pressed against his chest. As he stared at the man in front of him, he reached for the pistol he had tucked into the waistband at the small of his back.

Jack watched the man intently, sensing he was up to something.

"Hand over the laptop, Rourke. There's nowhere for you to go. Greenberg is dead, the mansion is under our control. Your only option for getting out of this alive is to hand over the laptop and put an end to this. No one else has to die today," he said.

"Maybe just one more," Rourke said, producing his pistol.

Jack fired three times without hesitation. The first bullet struck the laptop dead center, sending it spinning from Rourke's grip. The second round hit Rourke in the chest where the laptop had been, sending him staggering back a step. The last bullet hit its mark right between the man's eyes snapping his head back in a mist of blood.

Completely ignoring the man who now lay motionless on the ground, he calmly walked over to the laptop, picked it up from where it lay partially buried in the sand, and opened it. The bullet had shattered the innards; he doubted they would be able to retrieve anything from it.

It was over, finally.

———

Berg woke with a huge throbbing pain in his chest.

The Kevlar body armor interwoven with titanium thread had saved his life. He looked up, trying to get his bearings, instantly realizing the mission had gone south when he saw the targets down at the water's edge.

Common sense told him to retreat, report back to the Hierarchy then regroup for a later battle.

Gingerly he got to his feet, stealthily leaving the scene unnoticed. Within moments he had hot-wired a Land Rover Discovery that belonged to the mansion and had driven off down the drive. He would report the situation and see what his new orders would be once he was clear.

He felt no enmity towards those he had fought against, it was just another job. This one had not turned out as he had expected, but he put that down to the caliber of opponent rather than to any shortcomings he or his team had. It was a rule in battle to never underestimate your opponent, this had been his only mistake, but it was one he would not repeat.

CHAPTER FORTY-TWO

"Did you get anything from that laptop?" Bainbridge asked Deakin.

He was anxious to see what progress had been made, if any, with the recovered laptop. The tech wizard had been working on the damaged laptop in his possession since they had returned from Scotland over four hours ago.

A clean-up team had been called to take care of the carnage they had left at the mansion, but no sign of the giant mercenary had been found anywhere at the scene. He had simply vanished along with one of the Discoveries from the garage. They had been a little surprised to find no traces of blood where he fell and realized he must have been wearing body armor.

"Nothing, I'm afraid, sir. The hard drive was completely fried. After being immersed in the seawater and then being ripped apart by a bullet, there was nothing left to recover. I can tell you that we were able to discover that they were trying to set up a stable uplink to a satellite that would allow them to download the NOC list to any server on the planet but..." Deakin said, pausing.

"But what, man, spit it out," Bainbridge urged impatiently.

"Well, sir, they failed. They didn't manage to connect to the uplink. The NOC list remained on the laptop, it went nowhere," Deakin explained with a flourish.

Bainbridge took a step back, relaxing a little. After everything they had gone through, continually having the Hierarchy one step ahead of them all this time, he never expected a break like this. This was like winning the lotto.

"Thank you, Deakin. Good work," adding as he turned to leave. "Dispose of that laptop, please. I want nothing of it to remain, is that clear?"

———

Once settled in a small innocuous hotel room in London, Berg rang up his contact in the Hierarchy. He was not used to failure. This call he had to make was going to be as unsettling for him as it would be for the Hierarchy to hear.

"I was unable to complete my mission. The opposition was too good. As for the rest of your plan, I have no idea how that turned out," he said once his call was connected.

There was a pause on the line; he suspected his contact was too angry to reply.

"That is unfortunate, but you will have a chance to redeem yourself. Keep your phone on, I'll be in touch," the voice said, abruptly ending the call.

———

Tony stood at the foot of the sterile utilitarian hospital bed, looking at the figure occupying it.

He had accompanied Mike to the small private hospital. The Service used it specifically for situations such as this. Tony had remained, nervously pacing in the waiting room throughout the long surgery, anxiously awaiting updates from the doctors. The prognosis was good; he would make a full recovery but would need some time to recuperate. SI6 would be short-staffed, but they would survive.

The door opened and a tall figure entered wearing a white coat.

"How long before he wakes up, Doc?" Tony inquired.

"It could be anytime now, Colonel," replied the doctor. "We repaired the damage from the bullet and set the broken bones, he should be okay soon, but he'll be more than a little sore for a few months. I hope you aren't thinking of putting him back on active service just yet. He'll need at least six months to heal properly."

"Can't you see a guy tryin' to grab some shut-eye here?" Mike said in a gravelly voice.

"Sorry, Mike," Tony said quietly as he walked closer to the head of the bed.

"How do you feel?" he asked.

"How do you think? I was shot and crashed a chopper. I feel like shit, Colonel, sir," Mike said, grimacing through the pain.

"I'll let you rest. I'll look in on you later and tell Bainbridge you're awake," Tony said, turning to leave.

"You never answered my question, Colonel," the doctor reminded, blocking his exit.

"It's not up to me, Doc, you know that. I give you my word though, I'll do my best to give him the time he needs, but you know as well as I do that sometimes these events don't play by the same rules we do." He pushed past the medical professional, tossing over his shoulder as he left, "I'll be back later, Mike, get some rest."

———

Jack stood outside the front door entry of his home for several moments, working on composing himself before entering.

Debriefing at HQ had been quick and not as in-depth as usual due to the fact Tony and Bainbridge had been present at the end of things and were able to corroborate most of what he reported.

What stopped him from entering was the unknown; how would she greet him on his return? To her, everything was very black and white—he had not returned when he said he would, to her, that was as good as breaking a promise.

Steeling himself, he opened the door and entered his home.

She was standing at the sink. Hearing him approach, she turned and looked at him.

With one simple look, he knew everything would be ok.

She smiled, walked up to him, and threw her arms around his neck, hugging him like she never wanted to let go, ever.

"I thought I'd never see you again," she said breathlessly.

"It's over now, baby. I'm done," he replied.

"Daddy!" squealed a small voice from upstairs, quickly followed by the rumble of tiny feet as his young daughter bounded down the stairs to join them in a family-sized group hug.

A knock on the door interrupted the family's reunion. Jack reluctantly pulled away from his wife and daughter, "Wonder who that could be. Put the kettle on, lover," he said with a smile, "I could kill a brew. I'll go see who that is."

CHAPTER FORTY-THREE

Berg had been waiting outside the Cross home ever since he had received the call with his new orders.

He had been waiting outside the door since shortly after he had seen Jack enter the home. If this was to work as he wanted, he needed the element of surprise on his side.

Let them relax for a few moments; let them lower their guard, and then he would act. They would not be expecting anything this soon after him coming home.

He knocked on the door, listening closely, bracing himself as he heard footsteps approach from the inside.

———

Jack had barely cracked the seal in the doorway when it burst open, throwing him back a few steps.

"What the—"

Before he could react, a huge man barrelled through the open doorway, his large shoulders nearly brushing each side of the doorframe.

Massive hands grabbed the front of his shirt, moments later, he was airborne seconds before smashing into the wall. Pictures crashed to the floor from the impact.

Stars danced before Jack's eyes as his head smashed against the brick wall.

He would have fallen when his legs buckled had it not been for the giant holding him aloft, glaring into his unfocused eyes with evil intent.

"You interfered with Hierarchy business, and for that, you must pay," Berg spat through gritted teeth.

Screams erupted from the kitchen where Melissa protectively held their daughter back, both terrified by the sudden intrusion.

The giant glanced their way, a cruel smile crossing his face as he looked at them.

Jack mustered all his waning reserves of strength, grabbing the hands holding him and twisting his entire body in an attempt to break the hold.

His effort was punished by being unceremoniously smashed against the wall with even more force, rattling his teeth inside his skull hard enough to shake his fillings free. Once more, he was airborne as he was thrown down the hallway towards the kitchen, landing hard on the carpeted floor.

Jack's eyes went wide with fear when he turned to see Berg holding a pistol and registered that he was aiming it, not at him, but at his family down the hall.

Two shots rang out, he watched helplessly as his wife and daughter fell, one after the other, to the kitchen floor.

Rage erupted within him as he retrieved his own Walther from his waistband.

Twisting back towards the giant, his own gun

extended, he barely had time to hear the giant mutter, "Shit!" before a rapid double tap on the trigger placed two bullets in the middle of the forehead of the man who had just ripped his world apart.

Berg's head exploded as the bullets smashed through his skull, painting the wall directly behind him, and the force of the bullets' impact propelled him backward until he collided with the door. Momentarily the giant stopped, already a corpse, before his body slid to the floor, leaving a trail of blood and gore.

Jack unsteadily got to his feet, dreading what he would see as he went to the kitchen entrance. He looked down at the bodies of his family as they lay suddenly silent. His legs gave way, refusing to support him as he slipped down the wall crying out in anger and grief. Tears began to flow freely as his disbelief at how his world had changed so suddenly overwhelmed him.

He looked at his hand through eyes swimming with tears, he still held his gun.

Without Melissa, he didn't want to live, didn't think he could live.

He placed the muzzle under his chin and gritted his teeth, nothing happened. God, he wanted to die. He couldn't face life without them, but he couldn't bring himself to pull the trigger either.

In anger and frustration, he threw the Walther across the kitchen.

Drawing in a shaky breath, he slowly took his phone out of his pocket and dialed Tony's number.

EPILOGUE

Tony sat before Bainbridge, looking down at his hands that held a tumbler containing a decent measure of Macallan Whisky.

Both men were still in shock after Jack's call. Naturally, they had taken swift action, personally taking care of the details. A team had been sent to clean up the house, the bodies of his wife and daughter had been properly and respectfully seen to, and finally, Berg's body had been disposed of in an incinerator the service used for occasions such as this.

In a few short hours, the operational capability of SI6 had been decimated.

"What happens now, sir? I mean, where do we go from here?" Tony asked.

"Where do you think? We go on, of course," Bainbridge said in a matter-of-fact manner.

Tony looked at the General, whose expression was one of stoic solidity that often gave the impression that the man was uncaring. Tony knew differently though, it was simply that the General's job made it difficult for him to show his feelings. He had to make incredibly tough decisions that often put operatives in harm's way. He would never be able to carry out his job if he allowed his feelings.

"Seeing as how Jack is grieving a huge loss and Mike is in the hospital for at least another three months, and we know as much about the Hierarchy now as we did at the very start, which by the way, is about fuck all, excuse my French; if they should decide to do anything, I doubt we could muster up enough manpower to fight them."

"You worry too much, Tony. You let me worry about staffing problems; I have a few ideas up my sleeve."

Tony drained the amber liquid from his glass; looking at his boss, he placed the empty glass on the desk.

"You have someone already lined up, don't you?"

Bainbridge almost managed to hide a brief smile. "I knew this situation would come at some point; it's always good to have a backup plan, you know that," he said.

Tony smiled. He should've known Bainbridge would not allow something like the depletion of his personnel to hamper his performance. He thought sombrely for a moment about Jack and what he was going through. "What do you intend on doing about Jack?" he asked.

"I'll extend all the help I can as long as he works for this department. After that, it's out of my control. What I won't do though, is pressure him, not yet anyway. When I think he's ready to return to work, I'll extend a hand to him, but at the moment, we have to give him time to heal, the same as Mike. Until then, I'm quite sure who I have in mind can fill in for them both."

Tony stood up.

"Well, if that's all, sir, I think I'll retire. It's been a hell of a day, and I have a feeling tomorrow is going to be just as hectic," he said.

"No, that's fine, Tony, you go get some rest. I'll be heading off shortly myself," Bainbridge agreed.

With a nod, Tony left the room.

———

Jack walked through his front door and stood frozen in the hallway.

Every trace of his attacker's blood had been removed, as had that of his wife and daughter. It was surreal, as if nothing had happened.

He had to pretend as if everything was normal until the story that had been fabricated about their deaths in a motoring accident while he was away was released. Sometime tomorrow, it would be reported that their bodies had been found near the site of the accident, moved to a safe place for internment, and the story would be released. Until then, he was expected to act as normal as possible.

How in Hell was he supposed to do that?

He walked to the end of the hallway, standing a few long moments at the bottom of the stairs that led up to the bedrooms. Without looking at the kitchen, for fear of seeing them still lying there in their own blood, he walked methodically up the stairs to his bedroom.

As he sat on the edge of his bed, he thought about how it had happened. What had the assassin said? He had interfered with Hierarchy business and that had to be punished...or something along those lines.

He may have interfered with their business, but they had stolen his future, his life with his family, and that would not stand.

He quickly realized he could not move forward with his life until this matter was resolved; how could he, knowing that those responsible were still out there? What could he do?

He had no intel on them, not even the slightest idea of where to begin. Right now, he was powerless to do anything.

What would his wife say about this? Ah, yes, he knew exactly what she would tell him. In his mind, he could hear her voice telling him she would not want him tormenting himself over this. That he should put this behind him and move on with his life, and that, above all, she only ever wanted him to be happy, and seeking revenge would not make him happy.

He needed time to think. He needed to allow the grieving process to run its course. Until then, any decision he made would be colored by his overwhelming grief.

He went through the routine of getting ready for bed as though on auto-pilot and crawled between the sheets of the bed they had shared.

Yes, he would take the time he needed and then make the decision.

Sure, sleep would not be within reach tonight. He closed his eyes and thought of his wife.

Tears welled in his eyes as thoughts of Melissa, their daughter, and happier times filled his mind, but exhaustion from the recent events took their toll, and he drifted off to sleep.

ACKNOWLEDGMENTS

I would like to thank everyone who has helped me along the way. My family, obviously. Without their support. I wouldn't be able to do this.

A LOOK AT BOOK TWO:

Crosshairs

The need for revenge is deadly, and the stakes are sinister...

Jack Cross and the rest of the Special Intelligence Section Six team are back, and the Hierarchy for Anarchy Terrorism and Extortion is out for blood.

They want revenge on SI6 for their intervention in stealing the NOC list. And this time, the mission is personal. As the Hierarchy takes step after step to destroy SI6, Jack realizes that this corrupt order is determined to win—no matter the cost.

With a battle raging on all fronts and across the world, these two elite organizations collide in a battle so fierce that lives are lost and life as they knew it...will never be the same.

AVAILABLE MAY 2023

ABOUT THE AUTHOR

Jack Dillon loves to write fast-paced thrillers that have plenty of action. He grew up watching James Bond films, and he read every one of the books he could get his hands on. When other authors started catching his eye—authors such as Clive Cussler, Jack Higgins and, Matthew Reilly—they inspired him to write his own adventures.

So far, Jack has written two series with strong leading characters, the Jack Cross series and the ATLAS Force series. A statistic of the pandemic, he was forced into early retirement. But it wasn't such a bad thing as it gave him the opportunity to write full time, which had been a long-held dream of his.

Living in a beautiful part of the Derbyshire peak district, Jack takes advantage of the wonderful scenery. And when he isn't gazing at it through a window, he can be found finding other ways to procrastinate. Don't worry, though, he still has plenty of ideas that will eventually find their way into a book. At least, that's what he tells himself.